LOGAN

THE PRIDE OF THE DOUBLE DEUCE BOOK 5

KATHI S. BARTON

This is a work of fiction. Names, characters, places, and incidents are products of the author's imagination or are used fictitiously and are not to be construed as real. Any resemblance to actual events, locations, organizations, or persons, living or dead, is entirely coincidental.

World Castle Publishing, LLC
Pensacola, Florida
Copyright © Kathi S. Barton
Paperback ISBN: 9781629895321
eBook ISBN: 9781629895338
First Edition World Castle Publishing, LLC, September 5, 2016
http://www.worldcastlepublishing.com

Cover: Karen Fuller
Editor: Maxine Bringenberg

CHAPTER 1

"I've no idea." And he didn't as he sat there looking at the paperwork in front of him. Logan wanted to hand it over to his brother again, but Zach had asked him to come over and look at it and he was going to do that. But as far as knowing if it was a good deal or not, he wasn't sure what to tell his brother.

"To me the interest seems a little high. But then as Landon said, I only have this ground as my backup, and I've not made but two payments on it so far. And the first one was late because I forgot to take it to the bank while they were open." Logan handed the paperwork to purchase the tractor Zach needed back to his brother as Zach continued. "It wasn't really late, but I wanted to pay it on the day it was due, not the next day."

"You're going to hurt yourself overthinking this shit." Logan got up and pulled them both a bottle of water from the fridge before being seated again. "Okay, here's the way I see it. You only

5

get the interest charged to you when you drag out the payments for as long as this loan is for. I'd not pay it off too soon…there is the matter of you having no credit. But after a year, I'd pay it off and move on to something bigger. You'll more than likely need it the way things are going out there anyway."

"The family is buying the grain I raise the first three years. I can't sell to anyone else." Logan said he knew that. "And Jace is paying to have a barn put in, one that will hold all that I can grow, as well as the tractor."

"I've seen the plans. It'll be large enough to hold three of these suckers." He took a drink of his water, trying his best not to think of what was going on right under his ass with his own home; and to not be angry about it. He was angry a great deal lately, and wasn't entirely sure why. "I'm guessing that the work on your home will be finished before Christmas, right?" Zach said that things were moving right along.

When Logan had moved into the family house, given to him by his aunt, he'd had no idea what he was getting into. The furniture was all nearly new; the carpets were worn through in some places but in otherwise usable condition. And he had a roof over his head that didn't leak, so long as it didn't rain for more than three or so hours.

When the furnace, nearly as old as he was, broke down, he'd called in someone to fix or replace it. What they found was that not only was the furnace not worth saving, but the house would be, even with the installment of the new furnace, worth less than it would cost him to have the furnace put in. The foundation was shot.

Logan had to find someplace to live. He'd been told that with the age of the house, the way that it was out of date, and now the foundation, he'd be better off building new rather than fixing. He knew that in order to have a safe home he was going to have to start over or find himself an apartment in town and use the land for something else. What that was, he had no idea. He'd not decided on what he wanted to do yet. Moving away—out of the ranching business, the family business, and away from them all—was sounding better and better all the time of late. Not that he didn't love them, but he was bored out of his ever loving mind.

The man who had come out to talk to him showed him the way the foundation was slipping, and in less than five years, not only would the house fall in on the basement, but the waterlines were in bad shape, as well as all the electrical wiring. He told Logan that the wiring would probably burn it down long before the house fell, but there was little doubt that it would fall.

"How much longer are you going to be staying here? I'm to understand that you've been told to move out." Logan told him he was working on it. "It's really sad to see it go, don't you think? There are a great many memories here. And in the yard. I don't know that I'd be able to have it torn down either."

"I have someone coming in next week to pack everything up. You got what you wanted out of here, right?" Zach said that he had. "Jace and Mason are coming by later to get the rest of the things they picked out. And there are the pictures that I still have to go through. I've taken them to a storage unit in the event something terrible happens here. I never realized how many boxes there were."

"I don't envy you at all." Logan assured him it wasn't so bad. Zach stood up and stretched, and said, "Okay, I'm going

7

to sign the paperwork and have them deliver the tractor when it gets into town. I think they said five days from the time I get the money to them until I have it. But about the house, Logan…as I said before, you can come and stay with me should you want. That trailer that I'm staying in is pretty nice."

"I'm all right here. But I'll keep it in mind."

Logan sat at the table for another hour before he got up to make himself some dinner. The rest of the family, his other brothers that were mated, had butlers, cooks, and maids. He and Zach were the only two that had to make due for themselves. Logan wasn't sure, but he thought he might like his way better. Less people underfoot.

As he made his way to the ranch, riding old Sable, his horse, he thought of his days now. He'd been in charge of repairs, a daily thing, since before Jace had married. And since there was nothing old—not even houses, except his own, that were older than a few months old—his job consisted of taking hay out of a trailer that might be on the property and loading it in one of the many barns that held it for the cattle and horses. Or—and this one drove him nuttier than a fruitcake at Christmas—he was set to ride lines. Lines that a hundred other people working the ranch checked every day when they were out and about.

Frankly, he was thinking of taking a job in town, just to have something to occupy his mind rather than all the things he wished he could do. And just lately he'd been thinking of going into one of the barns and breaking a bunch of the new shit so he'd feel useful again. Viable, he thought. Because for all his family saying that they needed him around, Logan certainly didn't feel it. He felt like a fifth wheel.

"Just the man that I wanted to see." He looked at the tractor trailer in the yard that he could see was filled with bales of hay, and then back at Mercedes. "I think that can wait a minute or two, don't you?"

"Yes, ma'am." He tipped his hat back, wondering what she'd need him for. As far as he knew, she had several of the hands eating right out of her hand. "I do have an appointment at noonish with one of the builders. Do you think it'll take that long?"

"No. It's a matter of one of my pieces of equipment. Georgie said you might be able to help with the instructions." He said he'd give it a try. "I was hoping you'd say that. And so you know, I had no idea you could speak another language."

"I can when pressed." He could actually speak ten languages, not including a few that he was picking up from reading books — antique books that were older than Monroe — and he was good at math. Of any kind. She handed him a stapled together stack of papers that looked like photo copies of photo copies of a manual. "And this would go with which of your fancy new machines?"

"The portable ultrasound machine for the animals. Mostly for the horses, but I thought using it for the cows won't be much different if need be." He nodded and started reading the instructions while she explained. "I have read the English ones three times and I keep coming up confused. I think it was poorly translated. I'm not sure from which language, but I know it's not well done."

When she moved out of the room to speak to someone at the door of her offices, he picked up the oversized laptop looking thing and started comparing the steps to have it work to what he

9

was seeing on the machine. By the time she returned, not even half an hour later, he not only had it turned on, but the display screen was now in English and not the French it had been.

"This is wonderful. Thank you so much. How did you do it?" He explained how whoever had set it up had simply pushed the wrong button. "That's it? I've been playing with this thing for three days and you only had to change the language? Christ, I should have asked you sooner."

It was more complicated than that. There was also uploading the new software that hadn't been updated before it was sent to her, and turning on the links she would need to be able to read it in her office and out in the field. But he only shrugged when she thanked him again.

Logan made his way back to the overloaded trailer to start his day. He was pulling the first bale of hay off the trailer when Mason came to find him.

"I'd have thought you'd have more of this done by now." Logan said nothing but felt his temper rise. "Not that it matters. But I was wondering what your plans are for this evening. I have this meeting I have to attend in town and wondered if you'd go with me."

"Everyone else too busy?" He knew that he sounded bitter but didn't bother taking it back. "I don't have any plans. What sort of dress is required? I don't own a suit that fits anymore. And my other tux is at the cleaners."

He was snipping, and the more he said the more his voice took a nasty turn. By the time he talked about his tux and the lack of having one, he was nearly ready to leap at his brother and tear him apart. An overreaction, yes, but he just couldn't seem to control his temper of late.

"What's up your ass?" Logan just popped his neck but said nothing. "For the last week you've been biting and snipping at anyone that comes close enough to talk to you. Even Bonnie, who I might add you made cry. If you have an issue with one of us, you should tell us before you get hurt."

"You want to try and hurt me, Mason, then bring it on. I'm about in the mood to kick your ass all over this ranch." When Mason started to climb up on the hay with him, he looked at the doorway where someone had whistled at them. *To them* would have been a better description. It was more of a way to get their attention. Landon looked amused as he took his fingers out of his mouth.

"You boys got nothing better to do than beat each other to snot, then I'd like to borrow Logan for a minute or two first. I don't have time to hear his bellyaching any more than I do yours, Mason." Logan looked at Mason, who looked ready to commit murder. "Or I could just go on in and tell your aunt that you're out here making a mess of things when there is work to be done. I'm thinking you boys are still afraid of her even though you're grown men."

"What is it you want?" Logan cleared his throat and started again when Landon only cocked a brow at him. "I'm moving hay. Again. And probably will be tomorrow too, if you want to know the truth of it. Whatever you want, you'll have to ask the master here."

Mason looked ready to resume the fight that Logan had offered up to him. It was on the tip of his tongue to provoke him more, but Landon laughed. Logan stretched his neck again and got down off the trailer.

"We're not done here." Logan just nodded. If he was honest with himself and Mason, he had no idea why but he thought he'd actually love for Mason to hit him; a lot, and hard. He walked to Landon and told him he was free to help him. Mason continued talking as he walked to the older man. "Logan, when you get back, we're going to talk."

Saying nothing, Logan followed Landon to his truck and got in. It was walk away or have the shit knocked out of him. Mason wasn't a mean fighter...neither was he, but Logan wanted blood, and he didn't care if he had to shed a bit to get it. He was angry all the time he thought, too angry.

"You wanna talk about it?" Logan told Landon that he didn't. "Well, suit yourself, but you should know you keep it up and there is going to be some tarring and feathering going on. You've been making quite the name for yourself around here of late."

"I'm bored." Landon said he could see that. "And fighting with someone will make me less tense. I think. I'm thinking that I need to move on. The house, the land, the lack of jobs...it's taking its toll on me. And my well-being. All I want to do is just sit at home and stay there. Not have any contact with anyone at all. And I'm sick of doing shit jobs, Landon. I haven't done a damned thing worthwhile in a long time."

"What if I needed you for something that hasn't a thing to do with cows and horses? Heck fire, boy, I'm not sure that this'll be anything that I might like, but I'm bored too." Logan pointed out that he wasn't fighting with his family. "No. No, I'm not. Could, I suppose, if I wanted to be in the dog house with my wife, or on the outs with my daughter and son-in-law. I've been getting myself in and out of trouble like you have, and I think we need a plan."

As they turned down a driveway, Logan felt himself begin to relax. He rolled the window down, despite the cold of the air, and thought maybe he should get a new truck. Or at least something that he could drive around in style. Not that he could afford something like this vehicle, and he didn't need anything to get around in but his steady and sometimes slow horse. But Logan thought he might enjoy having something. When the truck stopped moving, he looked out the front glass, only just realizing that he'd closed his eyes, and looked at the house and barn.

"Is this the Martin farm?" Landon said it was and got out. Logan was almost afraid to join him. He'd heard stories about this place all his life. Most of them he knew were untrue, but to see this place now, he could almost believe them. The area surrounding the big house was unkempt and overgrown.

"You thinking about the ghosts that haunt it here? I been out here three times in the last month. I haven't seen a single darn one of them." Logan asked him where the Martins were. "William died about three months ago, poor old soul. He knew it was coming; had me out to talk to him a bit here and there. Then when he passed on, the kids stuffed Dolly into one of the nursing places where she is tied to a bed all day and only let out when it's feeding time. But she's getting out soon, I heard. Had a doctor say she was doing all right and able to get out to one of them assisted living places. I don't imagine that sets too well with them kids of theirs. They're a lot like my Dirk was. Everything is about them."

Logan knew that Landon and his wife still hurt about Dirk and what he'd done to them. He also knew that Katie was getting help, too, for her depression. Logan loved these two people like no one he'd ever loved before. His own parents had been gone for so long, he'd begun to think of them as their substitutes a long time ago.

"I'm sorry, Landon. I truly am. But I have to admit, I don't remember seeing anything about the Martins' children." He looked at Landon when he said nothing. "We helped them out last year. He got sick and we came to help him and his men out by picking grapes. I liked Mr. and Mrs. Martin, but like I said, the children weren't around then."

"Yeah, I remember that. Right proud of you for doing that too. But he never did recover from what had put him down. Heard tell that when he passed on the kids were so mad at him that they only did what they had to do to get him buried. Then when the will was read, they got rid of their Mom too. I've been to see her a couple of times." Logan said he thought they'd been friends of his parents. "Your parents, they did right by them. Even before you boys were coming along, they'd go over and help them out. Their own kids never did appreciate them."

"Why are we here then?"

Landon opened the front door to the house. Logan was surprised to see that the man not only had a key, but seemed to know just where the light switches were, as well as glasses in the cabinets. But when he pulled a pitcher of tea from the fridge, Logan asked him what was going on.

"Six months or so before William passed on, he called me over here to have a little talk. And some of his wife's pie. She couldn't bake one to save her life, even when she poured the middle of it from a can, so I knew when I got here that I was in trouble. He was dying even then, he told me, and needed my help." Logan nodded, sipping his drink. "Dirk was alive then. He'd been in trouble with something, like he always was, and I called William back to beg off. But he said that he wasn't long for this world and it would do him good to see me. So I packed myself up and came over. I found that in the three or four months since I'd seen him last, William had aged a great deal."

"His kids." Landon nodded and got up and brought them a box of cookies. Not the kind that was homemade, but ones that had been processed so much they were only cookies because some ad guy said so. "What happened when you got here?"

"He told me that he wasn't going to be around long, and that he needed to settle some debts up before he passed on. One of them being about his daughter, the one that he'd fathered when he was a younger man." Logan leaned back in his chair and said nothing. "I can see where your mind is going. You're thinking that I might should have stayed at home. And I might agree with you but for what I found out. She's gone; this girl died before he had time to do much for her. He found out about her too late. You knew her too, Logan."

"No, I don't think so. I told you, I didn't know his children." He watched Landon pull out some pictures from a worn yellowed envelope, and almost wanted to get up and leave when he handed him one of them. Even upside down, he knew the face when he held it. "Landon, whatever you think you know, I'd just as soon you tell me. Those pictures…you know as well as I that she was not a child of Mr. Martin's."

"But she was. A child he fathered long ago. An affair, he told me, one that he regretted the moment he did it, but for the child

15

he never knew. Mary Shafer, she was his little girl." Logan took the picture and held it but didn't look. He knew what she looked like as well as he knew his own face. "You and her, you were mates."

"Yes. We were. She was killed by a drunk driver when she was ten. We'd been in school together, hung out when we could. I knew when I saw her what she was to me, even as young as I was. I tried to help her, protect her, but that was out of my hands." Landon said he knew that too, William had told him. "I had no idea that William was her father. Not that it mattered to us who she was. We were just children."

"Yes, you were. Now, Dolly, William's wife, she knew who she was too. Even the mother. Dolly was a better woman, I think, than most would have been, and opened her doors to the child when it was apparent that her mother wasn't giving her the things that she and William had sacrificed to get her. Clothing, a better home. All the money he sent for her each month went to habits that weren't beneficial to her child. So when she was killed, little Mary was in his will too." Logan got up and paced the big spacious kitchen. "Logan, William knew who—"

"No. I don't want to hear it." Landon said nothing. "Whatever plan the two of you hatched up, it has nothing at all to do with me. Mary died, and I knew then that things like having a mate and a home life were gone to me. I've moved on. I had no choice, but that didn't stop me from grieving for her like I'd killed her myself."

"Have you moved on, Logan? On account'a, from where I'm sitting, you're stuck." Logan stared at the man who had been the father figure he'd never had. His dad might have been just like

16

Landon McBride, more than likely would have been right there with them in this room. But he'd died. "You're carrying around some powerful hurt now. Seeing the others get their own mates, them having babies. You're hurting, aren't you?"

Logan thought about shutting him up; the anger surged forward like a quick moving storm over his body. When he sat down again, Logan picked up the other pictures and thought of the little girl who had meant the world to him. He realized then that Landon was right. He was jealous of his brothers, and was letting it color his world.

"She and I were inseparable. We did everything together… skinny dipping in the pond not far from here, sneaking into the barn late at night. I'd bring her food and blankets. One summer she spent the better part of it in that big barn, eating what leftovers I could sneak out to her. I was never sure why she was there or why she wasn't getting enough to eat wherever she was from, but we had fun. I even brought her things in the house and washed them up when no one was looking." He knew that his aunt had guessed she was there, or that someone was, and had begun leaving things like extra chicken and bread on the counter for him to take. "Then one day, just like that, she was gone, dead because some bastard ran a stop sign and killed her at a crosswalk."

"He left it all to you." Logan asked him what he'd said. "The vinery, the house, barns. Even the wine making business, it's all yours if you want it. There is more than enough money to keep it running, forever if you wish. He said that he knew of all the men he had met in his lifetime that you'd make it viable and keep it going."

17

"I don't understand."

Landon pulled out another envelope and handed it to him. There was a copy of the will and a sealed, smaller envelope with his name on it. Landon pointed to the small colorful tabs on the side and told him to read that first. William Martin had named not just him in his will, but also his little girl, the one that had died all those years ago.

"I bequeath all my worldly goods and possessions to Logan Benson Douglas, a man of good standing and intelligence. I wish for him to run my winery, live in the house, and keep it going in the name of a child that we both loved. Mary Shafer, my daughter, would live here too but for my lack of sense."

"What did he mean by that?" Landon said nothing and Logan was afraid that if he did answer, he wasn't going to like it. "Landon, why did he leave it to me? You know, don't you?"

"His little girl was killed by her mother; the drunk driver was none other than her own mother." Landon leaned back in his seat while Logan tried to wrap that up in his mind. "You want to know more, you're going to have to read what he wrote you. But you should know that if'n you don't take the land and what he's given you, the kids will get it. And as much as it grieves me to say this, they're no better than my own son was, and this place will have condos on it by the end of next year. And you know as well as I that this is good farm land, and to have them plopping houses on it is gonna do nothing for your family's ranches."

"They butt up against each other."

Landon nodded. If he said any more or showed him anything else, Logan had no idea. When he came back round, the thoughts swirling in his head, he noticed that the sliding door was open to the deck off the kitchen and he could see Landon's booted feet. Getting up, Logan went to see Landon to let him tell him this was a joke. Not a funny one, but a joke all the same.

"You all right now?" Logan said he wasn't sure. "Yeah, don't blame you none there. There's a lot to take in. If'n you're ready for the rest of it, then I can give it to you."

"I'm not sure yet. What do his kids think of all this? By now, I'm sure that they know." He said that they did and were none too thrilled about things. "Are they going to give me any trouble? I mean, if I take this?"

"You already took it, son. The only thing you've not done is moved in. And that could be done lickety split." Logan told him he knew nothing of grapes and wine making. "I don't imagine that many do unless they read up on it. And there is the foreman that is taking care of things for you. Production has been going on, grapes were tended to. William has been gone for a bit, not even a year, but someone's been here all along."

Logan sat down on one of the deck chairs and realized that they were fairly new. Now that he thought on it, Logan realized that the kitchen seemed to be updated and clean. He wondered what he'd find should he go looking around the rest of the place. He asked Landon about it.

"He had it all taken care of. Most of the renovations, they occurred before he passed, but he wanted things to be prettied up for you. Dolly, she said to me that last time I was out there to visit her that that someone had been hired to come in and take out all the personal things and put them in storage. The house, the lands, they're all ready for you." Logan asked him why now. Why had he waited so long? "It was time."

19

CHAPTER 2

Charlie tried not to think about how tired she was. First of all, there wasn't any rest for the somnolent, as her grandma used to say. And secondly, she knew that if she even laid her head down for a single moment, she wouldn't get up again. Exhaustion wore on her like a wall covered in old paper.

When she heard her name called, Charlie moved to the other room and waited for the man there to get on with his complaints. And Cliff Yates had plenty of them, real and imagined. But despite it all, she really liked the old poop.

It was a game they played. Well, it wasn't a game and rarely was it play. She knew that in a few seconds he was going to get nasty with her, and she was going to give as good as she got. He'd fire her, as if he could, and she'd leave him to whatever had happened to him. Then an hour or so later, he'd call her in and ask her, politely this time, to help him.

"You have to come and help me, please." She stood there

stock still while she tried to think why he was changing up the game. "Come in here, I need to talk to you."

"All right."

Moving deeper into his room, she closed the door when he asked her to. When she did this, careful not to get too close to his cane he'd used on others before, she waited for him to tell her what was going on. Closing the door could get her fired; being too close to Cliff on his bad days when he'd not remember her was worse.

"Can you mail something for me?" No, she started to tell him, she would not. The last time she'd done something for one of the residents here, she'd nearly gotten fired. "It's just a letter to my grandson. I want to let him know that I want him to come and visit me."

She took it before she could think not to. "Mr. Yates, you know as well as I that I can't do this for you. Things have to go through channels, and people have to make sure that you're not.... Well, I don't know what they're making sure of, but I can't do this."

"Please?" She looked at him then, really looked. Mr. Yates looked like he was going to cry. And she noticed that he had two new bruises on his face that hadn't been there when she'd gotten here for her shift. "You can see right there who it's going to. And if it'll make you feel any better, you can read what I put in there. I'm just an old man wanting to see his grandson."

"Mr. Yates." He looked away then, staring out the window that had no view other than a brick wall on the other side. Charlie looked down at the name on the envelope and wondered who Gerard Douglas really was. And why, after all his time in this place, did he want to see him now?

"They won't let me make any phone calls. And every time I try to mail out even a card, all I get for my effort is it coming back to me all torn up. It's a letter, nothing more, begging someone to come and see me." He looked at her. "I'm dying, child. I want to make amends before I go. And I have things I need to have taken care of. I need you to do that for me. As my only friend."

She was going to get into so much trouble over this, she knew it. Stuffing it into her uniform, Charlie told him she'd try and get it out. He sobbed then, holding his hand over his mouth so that no one would hear him. Just as she was ready to leave him, the door to his room was slammed back against the wall and there stood the meanest person she knew...Ben Mann, her boss and the residents' biggest tormentor.

"You've been told not to shut the doors to the rooms. How the hell are we supposed to make sure that they're not pissing in the corners if you keep breaking the fucking rules?" Charlie said she'd not shut it, it swung closed on its own. Just to prove her point, the door started moving closed again. "What are you doing in here anyway? Didn't I order you to go over to the west wing and clean that room that Mrs. Martin died in last night?"

Her heart twisted up again when she heard the news. She'd been one of the sweetest, kindest people she'd known. And when Charlie had come into work today they'd told her that she'd died. It had surprised her a great deal, as Dolly was saying how she was going to leave soon. And that she had a nice place to go to in one of the most expensive assisted living places in the state.

"I cleaned it up. And I'm about to head home." Ben told her she wasn't going anywhere, that she was going to do what he

23

said when he told her or else. "But I am. I've been here for nearly nineteen hours, and I should have been home a long time ago."

"You'll go when I tell you I'm finished with you. And you'd better not be expecting any overtime pay for this either. When you're needed, you'll damn well work." She said nothing, needing the job desperately. "Get the trash picked up and these creeps in their beds. It's almost dinner time."

By the time she was leaving, having just clocked out to go, she knew that she couldn't come back here. The place was just too depressing and the management staff were all pricks. Charlie was going to have to find something less stressful that didn't work her nearly eighty hours a week. As she was passing by Mr. Yates's room again, he waved her in and she stood just inside his door in his room and said nothing. If Ben caught her now, she'd be here for another twenty hours. Mr. Yates seemed to understand and spoke to her without his usual screaming for help.

"You gonna mail that for me?" His whisper was so low that she had to concentrate on what he was saying. "You will, won't you? And if you don't come back tomorrow, I won't blame you. I'll miss you something terrible, but I'd understand."

"He's killing me." He nodded and handed out his cookie on his tray. "You should eat it. You know that they count your food intake."

"One little cookie ain't going to make a hill of beans in the long run." She nodded and took the cookie. "Now go on and get out of here before he finds you. Be careful, child. You're the best thing that has happened to a lot of us in here. Even though I'm meaner than a snake to you, you should know that it's to get him to put you in here to clean."

24

She was nearly home when she remembered the letter. Taking it to the post office box on her corner, she stood there for several minutes, trying to decide if this was the right thing to do. Opening the blue box, she dropped it in the slot and then checked twice to make sure it went into the darkened box. Making her way the rest of the way home, all she could think about was that Gerard Douglas had better come and get his grandfather before Ben killed him.

Making dinner proved to be difficult. The water had been shut off...again. And when she asked the landlord about it, he told her that she was lucky that they had electric for what she was paying him to live there. When she started to point out that she wasn't paying him anything, but the people that owned the building, he slammed the door in her face. Going back to her little one room place, she pulled out her stash of water bottles and made some noodles with butter on them. That was about all she could afford right now.

Who would have believed that only six years ago she'd had not just a good job that paid her very well, but a house, a car, and money to burn? Then one day her boss, who she thought was a nice guy, came into the offices and shot the place up. He'd killed three of her co-workers and then himself before it was finished. It had been the longest eight minutes of her life.

Embezzlement, drugs, and money laundering had been on the short list of things he'd been in trouble for. There had been accusations that he'd stolen art from the museums around town. The people she'd worked with, herself included, were named in his confession as being in on his scheme. That each and every one of them had taken money from him when he'd done some deals.

It had taken Charlie nearly four of the years since then to clear her name; and with that, all of her money was gone. No one, not before or since, would hire her in her field. It seemed that they believed a dead man over her word in this.

Underpaid and overworked, she'd had to work shit jobs since then. Twice she'd been fired when things came up missing. Two more times she'd been let go for downsizing. She'd been a dishwasher, maid, and waitress. As well as a cleaning woman in a hotel chain and a short order cook for a dive. None of them had brought her from the brink of devastation.

Crawling into bed, she thought of Mr. Yates. He'd pretended to dislike her so that she'd be assigned his room to clean up. That had to be one of the strangest and sweetest things anyone had ever done for her. Still, going back there, even if she only worked an eight-hour shift, was going to be the death of her. But Charlie knew that she'd go, if for no other reason than she liked some of the residents that lived there. Especially Mr. Yates.

When her alarm went off at six the next morning, she was getting ready before she remembered that she was quitting. By the time she had on her uniform and her shoes tied, Charlie knew she was going to give her notice. It was more than likely going to get her fired, but she could not do this anymore.

Even though the management staff was supposed to be to work by seven-thirty, Charlie knew that Ben wouldn't be in until well after ten. She took her assignment from one of the equally overworked and overstressed nurses and made her way to Mr. Yates's room, the first one she was cleaning. He was sitting in the bed still and he'd not had anything to eat. Going to run down his breakfast, she was told that he'd been a bad boy overnight and wasn't to have any. But Gale, the day cook, handed her a box of cereal and a carton of milk even as she told her that he deserved what he got. Getting the food to the man nearly got her in trouble again.

"Where are you going?" She paused and looked at the clock over her head. It wasn't even eight yet and Ben was there. She turned to ask him what he meant. "Where are you going? I'm pretty sure that even you can figure out what that means when I ask you a question. Where are you going?"

"I'm cleaning the rooms." He glared at her. "Did you not want me to clean rooms? If not, I can go home."

"You'll get your ass in there and get those rooms spotless. There are some inspectors coming in today, and I'll not have you mouthing off to them either." She assured him that she wouldn't. Charlie had already done that on the website that they'd set up to talk about nursing home conduct. Never hearing from them again, she figured that like most things in her life, it was a lie. "And you won't have to worry about the mouthy ones either. I've taken care that they'll be nice and asleep when they get here."

"You drugged them?" He just smiled at her, and she was so stunned that she turned and went back to Mr. Yates's room. Closing the door, a no-no that would get her into trouble again, she handed him the food that she'd been able to get for him. While she was cleaning up his room, Charlie told him what she'd found out.

"They'll do me next, you can bet." She told him she was sorry. "I am too. I got me a thing or two to say to them people. Here, help me up. I got me a plan and you're going to help me. Keep them out for me, just a few minutes."

27

She helped him to his chair and then cleaned up after him. When the nurse came in to tell him it was medication time, Charlie asked for a few minutes, saying Mr. Yates had to go to the bathroom.

"You're gonna get me in trouble." Mr. Yates told her he had her back. When he handed her a small thumb drive, she looked at it, then him. "What's this?"

"You slip it to one of them inspectors when they get here. It'll tell them what they need to know." She tried to give it back to him. "No, this is our only hope, Charlie. It's gonna get their attention. They done went and murdered Dolly and those others that had money. It took me some doing too, to get that thing the way I wanted it. Never had so much fun working one of them old computers as I did with that one. You know that when you give it to them, they're going down for the murder of my dear Dolly."

"What do you mean?"

The door opened again and she was told to get out. It wasn't until she was in the hall that she realized she still had the thumb drive. She was so fucked right now.

~~~

Emma wanted to find her mom and tell her something was wrong. But she knew that she'd feel stupid if she did that and her mom would tell her that it was nothing. It had happened twice now, the false contractions making her feel like she was in labor. Sitting in a more comfortable position on the couch, she tried to concentrate on what was going on in front of her. The television had been muted but the program was no less interesting. Then another pain tore at her.

The door to the back of the house was opened and there stood

28

Monroe. Smiling at him even though she thought she was going to die right then, he grinned back. Putting her hand to her belly, she tried to stand up but fell back when she hurt again.

"I would have called my mother had I been you." She told him it was a false alarm. "I think not, Emma. You're well on your way to having your baby today."

"No. I have another week and a half to go. We still have to put the crib together, and then there are new baby things that have to be washed." He helped her to the floor, where he told her she'd be more comfortable. "Have you looked at me? I'm as big as a whale...I'm never going to get comfortable again."

"You'll see." He handed her a pillow and asked her about the television show she was watching. "I haven't seen much in the way of programs in a while. There is much to learn on them, I'm to understand."

Her father came bursting in the room much like he did everything. Monroe didn't even flinch, and she had a feeling that he'd called him here. As he made his way to her, her dad was talking a mile a minute. Most of which she did not understand.

"I'm telling you that things just get out of hand at times, don't they? Like a week ago, I had me this steer just where I wanted him and bam, he goes and charges at me. Hadn't been for Logan being there, I might have been hurt bad. I had a cupcake from the kitchen, in the.... We're gonna have to move you to your room, darling." A scream tore from her when Monroe picked her up with her dad's help. "Oh my lordy, put her down, put her down."

She hurt now; not just her belly, but she swore her pussy was coming apart. When Monroe told her to breathe, she let out a long breath that she'd not realized she was holding. Then she

29

sort of fuzzed out, because the next thing she knew, Mason was there and he was telling her to hold on.

"I hurt." He told her he knew that, that they were bringing in Mercedes. "She's a vet, Mason. I think I'm having our baby, not a horse or a cow."

"Yes you are, love. And Mercedes is going to help us. You're never going to make it to the hospital." When he told her to breathe again, she tried to concentrate on doing just that. When she heard her name, she looked into the eyes of her newest friend, Mercedes.

"You sure do like to cut things close." Emma wasn't sure what she was talking about, but didn't get a chance to ask her when another pain took her breath away. "Breathe, Emma. You need to breathe until I can have a look at you."

She was naked then. A blanket, warm and soft, covered her and Emma closed her eyes. To say that she was hurting now would have been grossly understated. She felt like someone was trying to kill her. Emma looked at Mason when he said her name.

"Your mom isn't going to make it." Her fuzzy mind thought he meant she was going to die, and she asked him to save her. "No, honey, she won't make it here for the birth. Mercedes is going to deliver our baby for us, and then you'll go to the hospital."

"Daddy?" She looked around and saw him outside on the deck, and looked at Mason. "He's afraid I'll die, isn't he? My dad is out there because he's afraid for me."

"That's some of it. You told him to get the fuck away from you and not to touch you." She denied it. "He's all right with being sent away, I think. One more scream from you and I think he would have gotten his gun out and shot one of us."

"Daddy always was very protective of me." The pain came in hot short waves now. There was no time to rest now…her breathing even hurt. "Mason, I don't want to have this baby now. I had no idea it would be so painful."

He laughed and she wanted to smack him. But the next pain was different, more like pressure than simply pain. She looked at Mercedes when she said her name. Emma was having a hard time focusing on her and told her to stand still.

"I am. The next time a pain comes on you, I want you to bear down like I told you. Hard, and scream if you need to." She glanced at her daddy standing by the glass doors outside. "He'll not come in here. Jace is out there with him."

The next wave of pain came and Mason reminded her to bear down. Once she did that, screaming as loud as she could, everything seemed to come to a stop. Her body felt…. Well, her body felt weightless, and she knew that it was time. Bearing down again when Mercedes and Mason told her to, she felt a sort of pop and cried out.

"It's a girl."

The room seemed to have gotten brighter, the air cleaner. As she laid back on the floor, Emma tried to catch her breath. Her throat hurt from screaming. Even her fingers were a little stiff from squeezing too tightly on Mason's hands. And when she heard the little cry, then a louder one, she looked up again and Mason was holding a small bundle. Her baby, her little girl.

"Our daughter." He handed her to Emma and she pulled away the blanket. There she was, the prettiest little baby she'd ever seen. Emma held her to her chest as Mason kissed her over and over.

In the back of her mind she knew that things were being taken care of. Her body felt different now. No more pain for one thing, but she felt lighter. And exhausted. When she was lifted up again, she realized she'd fallen asleep and that someone had taken her baby. Asking Mason about it was too much effort at the moment, and she knew that he'd care for her. When she was in a big bed, much softer than the floor, she asked him where she was.

"They're weighing her up right now. Mercedes said she'd be right back with her." Emma nodded. "You did well, my love. I nearly didn't make it."

"I had no idea I was in labor all this time." She yawned. "Mom is going to be so disappointed. Monroe, he knew."

"Yes, he knew. And called us all to you. Your father, he was so worried that I was worried for him when you screamed." The door opened and closed and she heard soft voices. Then the bed shifted and she opened her eyes. "Here you go, Emma. She weighted a good nine pounds two ounces and is nineteen inches long. And I think she might be a little hungry."

It took her several tries to get her baby to her breast. Her body felt heavy again, like she was in serious need of a long nap. But Mason helped her, and once their daughter latched on, she knew things were going to be all right.

"We have to decide on a name, Mason. It's too late now for us to think about it any longer." He nodded and watched her nurse their baby. "Mason?"

"I know. But to be honest, I was hoping something would come to me before you had her. And I really needed those nine days, thank you very much." She smacked him again. "All right, but if you hate it, you have to tell me. Emily Kate Zelma Douglas. Too much? We could shorten it I guess. To just Emily Douglas."

"No." She felt tears fill her eyes. "Your mom and mine. It's perfect. They'll all love it. I'm so in love with you."

"And I love you too. Thank you for this. Our daughter. When you wake, you can shift and feel better afterwards." She nodded, still too in awe of the little creature in her arms. "I'm to tell you that your mom is coming with gifts. She and the others were in the mall when I called out to them. I think we might have to enlarge her room if this keeps up. I love you so much."

When Emily was finished, her little face relaxed in sleep, Emma curled the blanket around them both and watched her. As her own eyes got heavier and heavier, she realized that she was still at home, and told Mason that she didn't want to go to the hospital. He agreed, but he had someone coming to have a look at them both. She was too tired to disagree and fell asleep. In the morning she was going to show her baby off to the world. Emma yawned again and drifted off to sleep.

CHAPTER 3

Charlie sat in the big room and didn't speak to those around her. There had been an incident, the police had said to them. Then the police told the staff to go with them, and now they were all gathered in this room. There was trouble brewing for the nursing home because of an *incident*. Charlie thought that was a mundane word for what had happened.

Glancing up when there were black shoes in front of her, she looked at the officer that had sent them to this room an hour ago. He didn't look any happier than Ben had when the police showed up. Ben, she was sure, had more reason to be upset than this man did. Charlie thought perhaps someone's head was going to roll, and she only hoped it wasn't hers.

"Are you Charlie Stone?" She nodded and stood when he asked her to. Then she followed him down the hallway to one of the empty rooms. When they were seated, the two of them, she noticed an older man in the room with them. The cop started talking again. "Do you know a man by the name of Gerard Douglas? He's here to talk to you."

"No. I'm sorry I don't...yes. I mean no." He cocked his brow at her, something that she'd realized in the last hour he did very well. "What I mean is, I saw his name on something. A few days ago. But I have...Mr. Yates, he said he was his grandson."

"A letter." Charlie nodded. She didn't lie to the cops. It was one of her own unwritten rules. Sort of everyone's, she guessed, but hers was hard and fast. Nodding again, she told him that she'd mailed it out for him when he'd asked her to. "Mr. Yates asked you to mail a letter for him and you did. He claims that he gave you something else, too. That you were to give it to someone during the inspection."

"But he's...yes. A thumb drive. But I never got the chance. I was told to go to the lower levels and do the laundry before the inspectors got here. So by the time I made my way back up from the dungeon—what we call the laundry room—they were gone for the day, and so was just about everyone else. But I have it." He asked her where. "Somewhere safe."

"You were instructed to give it to someone else later then?" She said nothing this time. How he knew that was beyond her. "Mr. Yates, he left a note for you and the police, it seems."

Standing up, she staggered slightly and fell back down. The cop and the other man sat down beside her. Mr. Yates was dead; she'd been the one to find him this morning. They'd said it was suicide, but she knew that there wasn't any way for him to have hung himself. Not without a great deal of help.

"Tell me what you saw when you entered the room and found him there." Charlie closed her eyes and tried her best not to see him hanging there. "Charlie, I can't help him if you don't help me too."

"He was hanging from the hook in the ceiling. I think it was supposed to be for IV's or something like that, but no one could reach it that I saw. I don't even know how he managed to get up there to…he wasn't a frail man, but he was unstable when he walked. He was dressed in his dressing gown. Not a robe, he told me, a dressing gown. He had some very strange ways about him." She looked at the cop when he said nothing, then he nodded, as if to say go on. "I was told to start on his room to clean. I'd done it once already, but Ben—he's the guy that called you—he said for me to shut the fuck up and do it again. Like he wanted me to find him."

She knew he had. Not that she knew why, but she knew by the look on his face, the way that he'd been waiting for her outside the room. Ben had been leaning against the wall when she'd come out of the room, and it made her think he'd known just what she'd see when she went in there.

"Did he say why you were to clean someone's room twice in one day?" She explained to him why it wasn't twice. "Are you in the habit of working a thirty-six hour shift here? You do know that there are rules against that, right?"

"Yes, but Ben said that rules were for pussies. But it was forty-eight hour shifts most of the time. They're really short staffed since he had to fire three of the nurses and two orderlies when they didn't pass their drug tests when the inspectors were here. Do you think I can have some water? And a cookie? I didn't bring enough to eat for that many shifts."

He got up and went to the door and talked to the person on

the other side. The man sitting by her said nothing, but she could tell that he was upset. Charlie didn't really care, she just wanted to go home and grieve. Poor Mr. Yates.

"Did you know Dolly Martin?" Charlie turned and looked at the man again. "I'm Landon McBride. She was a good friend of mine. She was on this floor as well."

"She was a wonderful person. Much too lively for someone to have put her in here. She and Mr. Yates were friends of a sort too." He nodded as if he knew that already. "I'm sorry, but she passed away about a week ago. She…I was told that she died, but nothing else."

"There is a lot of that going on around here, don't you think? And I'm betting you know just what is going on, don't you, darlin'?" She just looked at her feet again. To have this day over with would be wonderful. When the officer handed her a can of soda, she declined it. Caffeine, she told him, didn't do well with her. It was replaced with a bottle of water, and she emptied it with one tip of it to her mouth. "You shouldn't have to work that much without proper care."

"It's not even good money, but I'm having a hard time keeping a job. Not that I'm a bad employee, but I have this thing on my record that makes real employers, the good ones, not want to have a second look." The elderly man asked her if it was a jail stint. "No. I worked for a firm that was in trouble. The man who… the owner blamed all of us for the things going on and it got in the papers. My name was with his, and people just assumed that I was as guilty."

A short knock sounded at the door and the cop got up to answer it. The quiet, because none of them spoke for a long while, had nearly lulled her to sleep. Charlie was tired and just wanted to go home to bed. But when a large, warm bag of food was set in her lap, her entire body woke up.

"Oh my, yes." Two burgers with everything on them, french fries, and chicken pieces. She looked at the officer and asked him what was hers.

"All of it. Eat it and when you're done, we'll talk." Nodding while she set up her burger, she ate the strips of chicken. Her belly rumbled with hunger, so much so that she had to let out a breath twice before she could pick up the thick hamburger and bite into it. "Not only should you not be working these kinds of hours, but they should be providing you with food and breaks too."

"Like I said, the money is crap but I really need the job. And I don't get hot food much. One thing or another at home keeps me from that." She took another healthy bite, not even caring if they laughed at her for her eating habits. "The place where I live, it has a burner, but the gas rarely works and the oven is scary. Last week the hot water was shut off…not for just me, but all of the complex. But it's cheap."

She finished off the second burger, leaving the fries alone. Not that she didn't care for them, she loved them, but the meat was what she knew she needed. When she leaned back in her seat eating the last of the strips, she asked the man what she was doing here.

"I mean, I thank you for the food. You have no idea how much I'm going to think about it over the coming days. But you know as well as I that you want something from me, and I'd like for you to tell me." The cop nodded. "Mr. Yates, he didn't kill himself, did he?"

"We don't think so, no." The cop glanced at Mr. McBride. "When he asked you to mail that letter to Gerard, did you read it? Did he tell you what was in it?"

"No, it wasn't addressed to me." She looked at both men then. "I'm going to lose my job over this, aren't I? I told him that I would get in trouble. The inmates...the residents aren't allowed to have things going out that Ben doesn't approve of first. But I did it for him because I really liked the old poop. But I have a feeling that he was fibbing to me. He said that Mr. Douglas was his grandson."

"I think you had it about right the first time. Inmates." Mr. McBride laughed, then looked at her sadly. "I'm sorry to tell you this, honey, but this place is going to be closed up by the end of the day. The inmates are going to be put into the hospital to be evaluated, then sent to other nursing homes to be cared for. More so than they ever were here. We think that Ben has been killing them for some time now for the income. The money from the state, as well as the money from some of the insurance policies that they have, names him as benefactor. Not in Mr. Yates's case. I think he just...well, we think Ben just wanted to hurt you by what was in the letter from Yates."

They asked her more questions, mostly to do with Ben and the other staff members. The man, Gerard Douglas, came in a bit later and just sat there with her. He said nothing but stared at her like she was a bug on the wall. Finally, he got up and moved around the room to sit in the window seat. When she was released, Charlie gathered up her things and went home. There were things she needed to get done, like find a job and figure out what to do next.

~~~

Gerard wanted to hunt down this Ben person and beat the shit out of him. Then when he was finished, do it again. As he sat there while they interviewed him again, he read the man's mind, which was as dark and as scary as anything he'd ever been in.

You all right? Howie LeBlanc, his friend and a good cop, had come along when he'd asked him to, just after he'd received the letter from Yates. *We can finish up here if you want and call in the other cops.*

He killed those people for no other reason than he wanted their income. What sort of sick fuck does that to people? Howie told him all kinds. *Yeah, well, I can't wait to get back home to my wife and the ranch. This guy is making me sick. And by the way, that other woman, Stone? His plans for her are less than nice. He has some drugs in his desk now that he was planning to slip into her lunch and rape her. The poor girl can't get a break either, it seems. Where is she, by the way?*

She left here about an hour ago. Gerard asked him why they'd let her do that. *I didn't. I guess she figured that we were finished with her and she wanted to go. You'd know that more than I would. I don't think she was involved in all this, was she?*

No. She had a feeling about what was going on, and had even posted on the local news web page when they did an article about it a few weeks ago. She didn't let them know who she was, but she was concerned enough to fill out the form anyway. She's going to need a job. I wanted to talk to her about that, but.... Christ, she's not had a good time over the last five years or so. Her living conditions alone are enough to make me think that she's just this side of being raped in her own home. She sleeps with a chair under her door so that people can't

41

get in. This Yates guy, he really liked her and wanted her to be taken care of. Gerard thought of the letter from Yates and the concerns he had, not just for his fellow inmates—he'd called them that as well—but for Charlie, and how she'd be hurt from this as well. *He knew that he was next on the list. Poor man said that he didn't want to die, not by Mann's hand, but he knew it was coming.*

That letter, you should let her read it. It might go a long way to getting her somewhere safe. Yates took a big chance getting that to you. Gerard nodded. *Do you know where this house of hers is? If so, I got this. With what you've given me on this guy, he's going to go to jail for a long time.*

Gerard and Landon left the nursing home. There were ambulances lined up out front, all of them taking care to make sure that the people they were loading were well taken care of. As he made his way to his own car, he asked Landon if he'd mind going to a less than desirable part of town with him.

"You gonna go and get that young girl?" Gerard said that he was. "Good. I'll be happy to go with you. And I got her a job too. After this, I'm betting that she's gonna need something."

"She's more than likely out job hunting now." Landon said he'd not doubt it. "Landon, that man Yates knew that he was going to be killed. And that this girl was going to be blamed for it. You heard Mann. He said that she'd been killing off the residents for months, but he'd not been able to catch her at it."

"Poor thing. And her just wanting to have food in her belly. Gerard, you should have seen her eat that meal he brought in for her. Howie told me later that he'd been gonna have him one of the burgers, but he saw the look on her face. I ain't once in my whole life been that hungry." They were driving to the address

42

that he'd gotten from her mind. "You thinking of taking her back to the ranch with us?"

Gerard knew that she mostly lived on noodles and butter, sometimes peanut butter when she could get it. Which wasn't often. Her rent wasn't much and her place was nothing more than a one room hovel that barely put a roof over her head. And all her extra money, all but what she needed, was going to taking care of her mother.

"Yes. But to be honest with you, I'm not sure she'll go. She's pretty stubborn." The both of them laughed. "Yeah, I guess she'd fit right in out there. Susie wants me to knock her out and bring her back anyway. Apparently she's already fixing up a room for her at the house."

Parking in front of the address, Gerard looked around the neighborhood. Christ, he didn't feel safe here, and he had an advantage over the people who lived here. Going up to the front door of the big house that looked like it needed to be condemned, he was nearly bowled over when Charlie came running out. Putting his hands on her arms, he felt her pain like it was his own. Setting her behind him, he confronted the man coming out the door after her with a whip in his hand.

"Can I help you?" Gerard stretched his neck, feeling the muscles there stretch with his cat. "You thinking of hitting her with that? Again?"

"Ain't none of your business. She's homeless as of right fucking now, and then she gives me lip. I'm going to take the sass right out of her, see if I don't." Gerard turned to her and saw the lash across her face. He asked her to go to the car with Landon. When she turned to do it, he turned back to the man. "You tell

43

her that she's going to pay for any damages too, see if she don't."

"I need my things." Gerard asked the man if he could get them. Of course, he told him no. "I have the things that belonged to Mr. Yates. The ones I was telling you about today."

"See? She's even a fucking thief." Before he could think of the consequence of his actions—or perhaps he did—Gerard hit the man in the face. As he went falling back on his fat ass, Gerard turned to Charlie and told her to get her things. And to hurry.

He and Landon went with her. Gerard wanted to tell her to leave her things, there wasn't anything here that she needed, but he knew that possessions, no matter how cheap and broken, were memories. Helping her gather her clothing and the few framed pictures that were in the place, he asked about the furniture.

"It's all things I've gotten at a secondhand place. I mean, I'm going to need them, sure, but I know that I don't have a lot of time to gather them up." He nodded and watched her face as she looked around. "It's all I have in the whole world, and now I have to start over again."

"Come on now, we'll get you going here before the police arrive." Landon moved her through the room. There really wasn't much here that he'd not have thrown in the burn heap. But Gerard watched her, knowing that he was going to help her even if she hated him for it. Smiling, he led her out to the truck and moved away just as the police were pulling in.

"If you could just take me to the closest hotel, I'd appreciate it. So long as it's a cheap one." Gerard could hear the pain in her voice. "I don't suppose you guys know of someone hiring, do you?"

"As a matter of fact I do. Gerard and I were just talking about

that." Gerard looked at her in the rearview mirror, and wanted
to go and beat the shit out of the landlord again as Landon spoke.
"You come on with us and we got something I think you'll like.
The pay is good too."

"I don't know about that." She looked at both of them.
"For all I know, you two could be mass murderers and I've just
stepped into your realm of hell. I mean, you were really nice at
the nursing home and picking me up.... Why were you picking
me up?"

"Howie said that you had the thumb drive." She nodded at
him but didn't look convinced. "If you don't like where we take
you, then you can leave. I'll even let you use this truck to go with.
So long as I get it back. I've grown kinda fond of it."

"Yeah, that'll work out so well. I'll drive away and the next
thing you know, I'll be arrested for stealing it. Just how stupid
do you think I am?" Gerard pulled over into the first parking
lot he found. "Are you going to beat me now? Or do you have
something more nefarious in mind?"

"No. What a negative mind you have. I wanted to talk to
you. About your life, who we are. What you're going to be doing
for Landon. He really does have a job for you. I don't know how
much you know about grapes, but my brother just inherited a
winery and he's needing employees. There really is a place for
you to stay. My wife is going to set you up in our place until you
can find one of your own." She said nothing, but he could tell
she was interested. "You've been hurt enough, don't you think?
There are shifters on the ranches, all of them. Myself, I'm a cougar.
However, Landon here is human. My brothers and sisters-in-law
are all cougars too."

"I know some shifters." He nodded at her, knowing that she knew quite a few of them. "You said ranch. What kind of ranch? Is it a slavery kind where you sell off human flesh?"

"No. Christ, you need more positive interaction with people. Horses for me. We raise and breed racers. My brother, Mason, has steer that he sells on the foot. My brother, Jace, and another brother, they have milkers. We have a dairy that makes cheese and other things to sell too. Zach has a farm; he grows some of the hay and other things we need to keep our animals fed. And Logan has a winery."

"You have five brothers?" He nodded and she looked over at Landon. "And this man? He's your...uncle?"

"Father-in-law to Mason, and good friend to all of us. Mason's wife is Emma, and they just had a baby girl." Landon handed her his phone, where Gerard was pretty sure there were about five hundred pictures of the little girl. When she handed it back to Landon, she stared out the window. "We're not going to hurt you. When Mr. Yates sent me that letter, I had no idea who he was. He told us what he thought, that Ben Mann was killing off the residents and why he thought he was. He also told us about you. He also thought that you'd be blamed for his death and those of the others that had died at the home. Mr. Yates wanted someone...me...to come and get you before it was too late."

"I'm sure he had plenty to say. I really will miss him. He was a pain in my ass, but one of the sweetest people I knew." Gerard said nothing. He could have told her Mr. Yates was worried for her, that he feared her having a heart attack because she worked too much. Or what he thought Mann's plans had been. He handed her the letter instead. She just stared at it without taking it. "He said I could read it when I hesitated to mail it for him. He told me that it was begging you to.... You're not his grandson, are you?"

"No. As I said, I didn't know him. He got my name from the paper. My wife and I, we have horses that we train. He got our name from there. Along with Landon's here. Mrs. Martin, she was a friend of Landon's, and when Yates talked to her about us, she apparently gave us a glowing recommendation to keep you out of harm's way." She asked him if she was going to be harmed. "He believed so. And I know for a fact that Mann had plans to rape you after he drugged you. He was planning to get you in the laundry room."

When she leaned back against the seat, he turned and started the truck again. He wasn't sure if she'd read the letter, but she had taken it. But he knew that she believed him about Mann and that Yates had been killed by him. He wondered, not for the first time in his life, what made people like they were. Simply mean bastards that enjoyed hurting people.

It took them over two hours to get back to the ranch. She never spoke to them again unless they asked her a direct question. Gerard didn't think of it as being rude…she was overwhelmed. He could feel every one of her emotions. As they pulled off the road and back to the house, she perked up but still kept quiet. As soon as the truck stopped, he turned to her again.

"No one will bother you here. You have free run of the house and the barns. The horses—Bride, especially him—will need to accept you before they'll let you near them. We have a vet here too…Mercedes, who is married to Darin, and they have a ten-year-old little girl." She nodded, not moving to open the door. "Charlie, you'll be able to come and go as you please. I promise you."

"I don't have a job. Nor money. I don't have but two pair of decent pants and four pair of underwear that would better serve as rags. Today was the first meal that I've had in a very long time that wasn't just hot but had meat in it." She looked at him. "You're offering me more right now than I've had in years, and I can't help but think that I'm dreaming or that someone is going to rip the rug right out from under me and tell me it was all a joke."

"No jokes, I promise you that." She nodded when Landon spoke to her. "My Katie, she's standing up there on the stoop. She wants to come on out here and hug you to pieces. I can see that look in her eyes. If you don't get out of here soon, child, she's gonna do it for you."

When she opened the door and got out, Gerard let out a long breath he'd been holding. She would be made welcome and she'd stay, but for how long was anyone's guess. As the other women in the household made their way to her, he thought of what had to be done here. She needed clothing and a place to work. He had a feeling that she wouldn't stay as a guest for very long if they didn't.

Can you come by the house? Gerard grinned at the sound of Logan's voice. *Mother fuck, I'm so screwed. The house just collapsed. It was like it figured out it was broken and went to great lengths to just say, fuck it.*

You hurt? Gerard started the truck to go to him. *I'm on my way. And Landon is with me, so don't be surprised when he gets there too. I guess you'll be moving now, right?*

I have nothing, Gerard. Everything I owned was in that house. He told him he was sorry. *Christ, it's a fucking mess and I — Shit.*

What is it? What's happened now? He told him to call the fire department, it just caught fire. *Shit. I'm coming. So are the rest of us.*

Reaching out to his family, he told them what had happened. As he was pulling away, he saw his aunt and the rest of them piling into their cars to follow. Even Charlie was being shoved into someone's car. He just hoped that Logan was all right.

CHAPTER 4

Logan opened up one of the lawn chairs that had been in the shed and sat in it. There wasn't a damned thing he could do right now but watch everything he had go up in smoke. What he had on, a dirty shirt and jeans, were all his worldly possessions as of right now, along with his hat and boots. His boots had been right beside him when the house creaked once, then started to fall in on itself, or he might have been barefoot out here. As it was, he didn't have a coat either.

Gerard pulled up first, then the other cars started to pull in. Logan didn't even bother getting up. There wasn't shit they could do either, and getting all up in arms about it wouldn't have done a damned bit of good. As the house burned—and it was going fast—he kept an eye on it so that it didn't leap to the empty barn and the shed on the other side.

"You okay?" He showed Mason the cut on his arm that he'd gotten when he'd had to crawl out of the basement at one point.

51

"You're just lucky that it didn't happen while you were asleep. You might not have gotten out."

"I almost didn't. Christ, it was like a nightmare. The roof made this sort of popping noise first. Then the walls just started falling in, right on my fucking head. I was running through the living room when I saw a large piece of wood slide through the television like it wasn't there. As soon as the floor collapsed under my feet, it was all I could do not to shift, and that would have killed me for sure. Then when I got in touch with Gerard I saw sparks, then the house went up like a pile of kindling." Logan saw the woman but didn't ask. There were people on the ranch all the time now. "I'm gonna have to move into that sprawling house now. I'm lucky, I guess, that I have it."

"You should come stay with us a couple of days, just to have the house cleaned out." Mason glanced in the direction that he was looking and smiled. "Her name is Charlie Stone. She's the one that Yates wrote Gerard about. She's looking for a job and a place to stay too."

"I don't have either of those for her." Mason just stared at him and Logan realized how nasty he'd sounded. "I'm a little stressed out. I nearly lost my life in my own fucking home."

The pop to the back of his head had him turning to see his aunt there. Aunt Georgie could cuss like a sailor when she needed to, which wasn't often enough if you asked him. She had a list of looks that could do a better job than a swift kick to your ass if you fucked up. The one she was giving him now was, I will beat you if you don't behave. He hugged her to him.

"I know you're stressed out, but there is no reason for you to talk like a longshoreman on leave." He told her he was sorry. "I think you should look on the bright side of this. Had we all been in that house, for any reason, we would never have made it out together."

He knew that. Aunt Georgie would have wanted to grab things to take. The rest of them would have been standing there trying to help her. It wasn't that she was a fool, but she had lived there with them forever and had memories too. He was lucky that he'd been the only one living there.

"You know how to clean up after yourself, so move into your home, grow some grapes, and make some good wine. You need to get out of the ranching life anyway." He looked down at his aunt. "I've seen you, Logan. You're bored out of your mind. You're fighting with your brothers and whoever else you can pick on. You think you have no value to them, and you're wrong. It's you that thinks that, not them. They depend on you for a great many things."

"I am bored; I will admit that to you. But the rest? I don't know, Aunt Georgie. I know nothing about wine. I don't even drink it." She hugged him and took his hand in hers. "Where are we going?"

"I want you to meet Charlie. Nice young woman who has less than you do. Perhaps if you two share stories, you'll stop feeling sorry for yourself and get to work." The fire truck pulled in then and he moved Aunt Georgie out of the way. The fire was still going, but there was no saving the house. But they did keep the barn wet so it'd not burn down too. He went with his aunt to meet the woman.

The closer he got to her, Logan felt his feet dragging. She was wounded. Not just from the physical cuts on her face and arm, but her heart. He had no idea how he knew that, but he could see it on her. She wore it like one would happiness…it showed on every part of her face. And when she turned to them, he saw her fight hard to bring the wounds back to her heart where they were and smile at them.

"It's gone up pretty fast, hasn't it?" He nodded at her, dumbstruck by her beauty. He knew he was making her uncomfortable, but he wasn't sure what to do about it. "My parents' house went up like this. But it was set. The fire department deemed it unfit to live in and they used it as practice. I don't think they thought it would go that fast, however. They had this all day event around this thing planned, and all they got to do was keep it from taking out the neighborhood too."

"They're gone?" She shook her head and looked at the house. "I'm sorry. I'm Logan Douglas. You came to work for my brothers."

"I suppose. Hopefully it's not here. I'm guessing that whoever lived here is going to be broke for a little while. But at least he has family to help him out. That's more than most people have when something like this happens to them." He looked to where she was looking and saw that while he had lost his house and contents, his family was here and safe. "That man, Mr. McBride, he said I can stay in the local hotel for a little while. Until I get my feet under me."

"No." Aunt Georgie and Charlie looked at him strangely and he realized how loudly he'd spoken. "What I mean is, you're going to work for me. At the vineyard. I just inherited it and the house is really big. Too big for one person."

"You think I'm just gonna shack up with you? I don't think

54

so." He shook his head, then nodded. "What is wrong with you?"

"I'd like to know that too." He looked at his aunt and tried to think what was wrong with him. "Logan, you should start over."

"Yes. Start over. What I meant to say was, I would like for you to come and work for me. I don't know what I'm doing. I know that I can figure it out, and there is a foreman that has been keeping things going for me. But, the house really is huge. Nine bedrooms with baths. A big eat-in kitchen with an equally big dining room." She asked him what she'd be doing in this big house with nine bedrooms. He liked her and smiled at her tone. "You could help me pick the grapes, if that's what I have to do. Taste the wine. I don't drink it, but I'm sure that someone needs to taste it at some point. And help me around the house. Not clean it, but just help out with cooking and stuff."

"And what else? Bed partner? I'm not into that." He asked her why and felt his face heat up when she looked at him again. "I'm not very good at it, if you want to know the truth. And I think it's a messy process too. Why people have it for pleasure is beyond me."

He wondered briefly if she was kidding. Then when his aunt cleared her throat and left them, he had a feeling that Charlie really did believe what she'd said. He wanted to ask her about her sex life, purely on an interesting fact finding mission, but he didn't. He just knew that she'd be too blunt, too graphic, and he wasn't sure he wanted that from her. Not right now, anyway.

"No, no sex." As soon as he said it, he realized that he really wanted to hold her. Touch her. Taking a step back from her, he told her again, no sex. Logan looked at what was left of the burning house. "This place, it was mine. My parents built it when

55

they first moved here, and I was going to have it improved but then I realized it was in bad shape. I was in there when it fell down. I'd had someone out a couple of weeks ago to change out the furnace, and he told me the foundation was going. I guess we're lucky it held on until we all moved out. Where are your parents?"

"My mother is in a nursing home. She's on a respirator as well as feeding tube. They said that she might recover, but I'm not sure after all this time. My dad is in prison. He was a drunk driver in an accident that left my mom like she is, and he killed a man and his wife." He told her he was sorry. "He's not a bad man. My dad worked hard, never missed work, and rarely if ever drank. But I'd just landed a good job, bought a house and car, and he'd been celebrating a little too much. He sits in his cell all day long and talks to no one, reads books that I send him, and refuses to see me but once a month. He said that he doesn't want me to tie my life up with coming to see him. Little does he know that I have no life, and nothing to tie me to one place."

"He blames you for all this?" She said no, he blamed himself. "But you blame yourself, don't you? You think that all this is your fault."

"I do, but he's ashamed of what he did, especially on such a happy occasion, and knows that it's me who is paying for Mom to be taken care of. It's why I need a job so badly."

Logan found himself wanting to help her. Not just with her having a job, but with it all. When the fire marshal came toward him, she walked away. He felt so bereft by it that he nearly begged her to come back.

"The house, as you can see, is a loss." Logan nodded. "I'm

56

sorry, son. I know that you kids were raised in that house. I don't know what I'd do if my parents' home did the same thing."

"I was lucky." He could see that he was now. And felt it. "My brothers had gotten out what they wanted in way of things that belonged to my parents. And I'd already taken the pictures and things I wanted to keep over to a storage unit that I have. So all things considered, it wasn't nearly as bad as it could have been. As you know, I was told a week ago that it had to be brought down."

"Yes. I know." They both looked at the men working to keep the embers from flaring again. "You got a place to go? If not, I'm sure we can make arrangements to put you up for a few days."

"I have a place. But I thank you." Logan watched Charlie; he didn't want her to leave him…leave the area. "I'm not sure what I'll do now."

Logan wasn't sure what he meant by that even as he said it. With the house? He'd call the insurance company and tell them what had happened, he guessed. The vineyard? He had a readymade job and home if he wanted. Or was it Charlie? Thinking of her, his cat stirred along his skin. She was going to be staying with him, helping him, and for whatever reason that made him feel like he could do this.

As things started to settle down he realized that he was starving. It was lunch time, he supposed, but looked at his phone and realized it was closer to dinner. And since all of his family had help to have their meals prepared, he decided that he wanted a big dinner that he didn't have to share with his family. Making his way to Charlie again, he waited until she was finished talking to Mercedes before he spoke to her.

"Would you like to have dinner with me? In town?" She asked him why. "Good question. I want to have something that I don't have to cook. Nor do I want to have dinner with my family. I love them, but right now I'd like to have dinner with a pretty girl."

"You going to invite someone else to join us?" He laughed, but he figured out quickly that she wasn't kidding. Nor did she know how beautiful she was. Rubbing his thumb over the cut on her cheek, he told her he wanted to have dinner with her. Logan wondered about the cut but didn't ask her. Not yet at any rate. "I don't have anything to wear."

When he got his mind and body to slow down on all the things that popped in his head when he thought of her naked, he told her that what he was wearing was all he had too. And if she'd join him, he'd take her by to see the house.

~~~

Charlie moved from room to room with Logan. They hadn't talked about this house over their pizza dinner. He'd told her very little about himself at all, actually. But she'd told him everything. She supposed, in a way, trying to make him realize that having her in his life was a mistake.

He seemed just as surprised by how much furniture was left in it as she was. Not only were the bedrooms all made up, sheets over the furniture to protect it, but there were linens in the closets as well as canned goods in the cabinets. She wondered how long it had sat like this. It couldn't have been long, she thought.

"I didn't know the man who left it to me, not very well at any rate. He had a daughter that I was in school with as a child. And when she died, killed by—well, she was killed—he knew what

58

we were to each other." She asked him what that was as they entered what had to be the biggest room she'd ever seen. "This is the master bedroom, I'm betting. Mates; she and I figured it out at a very early age. Anyway, he was her dad by an affair, I guess, and she didn't live with them; not from lack of trying on their part, however. Her mom was a piece of work, I guess, and he had no idea that she was his until later in her life."

The bed was near a bank of windows and facing them, so that the first thing the person who slept in here saw was the rows and rows of grapes. She moved to the window seat and sat down while he moved around the room. It was a beautiful view and she envied anyone that got to wake up to this every day. She'd bet it was even pretty in the winter. She watched the man walking around the long lines of fruit. Charlie felt the movement and knew that Logan was close enough to her to touch him.

"That's Mr. Roman Jingles. I asked three times, and yes, he's Mr. Jingles." She smiled as Logan sat beside her on the seat. "I've talked to him a couple of times. He speaks Italian and French, and English is only something he knows in passing. He has been trying to teach me a little bit about what goes on around here, but I've not paid much attention if you want to know the truth."

"I speak German, some. Fluent in French and Latin, but only enough of a few others to get me a taxi if I need one, as well as directions to the closest police station." He laughed with her. "This is a lovely home you have here. And I would like to work with you in the vineyard. I know nothing about it either, but I figure, like you said, there is someone here to help so we can learn until you don't need me anymore."

"I'd like that." He pushed the hair off her cheek. "Who did

this to you? I could have asked my brother, but I'd like for you to tell me."

"My landlord. He's not a nice person. I guess he's my former landlord now. Gerard, he and Mr. McBride helped me out of that place. I was going to have to leave anyway. I don't have a job anymore." He said that he'd heard that too. "Mr. Douglas, why do I feel so safe around you and the others? Is it a shifter thing? I mean, I've known other shifters—a wolf, a couple of bears—but I've never felt like this with them. Safe...not like you're going to lash out and hurt me at all."

"I don't know." He stood up when his phone signaled and smiled at her. "My brother, Zach. He wants to come by and borrow some Internet, he said. He has a computer at his house, but it's sort of spotty getting service. Zach has the grain fields. He's wanting to track a tractor that he just bought to see when it's to arrive."

Charlie followed him down the stairs. When he went to the front door, she made her way to the kitchen again. The pantry was filled with staples like flour, corn meal, and things like that, all of them in plastic containers. There were canned goods as well, and an entire shelf of the prettiest grape jelly that she'd ever seen. Moving from the pantry to the kitchen again, she was startled to find both men in the kitchen with her.

"I was looking to see what was in there. I didn't take anything." The other man smiled at her and Logan told her it was fine. They needed a list anyway. "There is no bread here that I can find. And there are freezers in there; one is stocked full of beef and one with chickens."

Logan opened the fridge. "We don't have much in here either.

We'll need eggs, bacon, and butter." He looked at her. "Do you want to make a list to take with you?"

"I'm going somewhere?" He asked her if she'd go to the store. "Sure. I don't have a car or any money."

"Here." He handed her his keys and a credit card. "I'll call the store and give them the heads up that you're going to use my card. Not that I think they'd give you a hard time. Just get whatever we need. There's plenty of money—"

"Okay, slow down here. You don't know me well enough to give me your truck or your credit card. For all you know, I could just take off and never return with either." He said he trusted her. "Why? Like I said, you don't know me."

"No, I don't. But I trust you." She looked at the other man, wondering if he thought his brother was nuts too. "Zach, this is Charlie Stone. Charlie, this is Zach. He's trying to track down his tractor, like I told you, or I'd take you. You can drive a standard, right?"

"Yes." Before she could think about what she was doing, she was out the door and in the truck. As she turned, using the directions that were given to her, all she could think about was these people were insane.

The store was just where they told her it would be. Armed with the credit card, the grocery list, and her own empty wallet, she entered. Charlie had never been so terrified in all her life. Someone was going to have her arrested, she just knew it. When someone touched her shoulder, she turned to look at the beautiful woman standing beside her.

"Charlie?" She nodded. "I'm Holly, Jace's wife. We met earlier. Are you all right? If you don't mind me saying so, you look completely out of your element."

"They sent me here for groceries." Charlie showed Holly the list. "I've never done this kind of thing on a scale like this. Not to mention, he just gave me his credit card and truck keys like he knows me or something. Or we're dating. I'm not dating him."

"Not yet." When Holly handed her back the list and grabbed a cart, Charlie followed her. "Okay, we're going to do this my way, because while you're new here, you don't know the store like I do. Not that I shop all that much, but I have been in here a few times to get something for our cook."

"Okay." As they moved along the dairy aisle, she asked about that. "Do you supply milk to the family? We have milk on here, so I'm assuming not."

"You know, I never thought of that before. Why don't we drink the milk that we raise? I'll have to ask. We do have cheese, so if that's on your list, mark it off unless it's something we don't carry." They went over the list and there wasn't any cheese at all. "Okay, milk and butter. Do you cook? That'll determine how much of that we'll need."

"Cooking at home is cheaper and better for you. So I guess I'll cook." She could, but rarely got the chance. They were standing in front of the sour cream and other things when she saw the yogurt. Charlie loved yogurt and wanted some in the worst kind of way.

"Get it, Charlie." She looked at Holly. "Get what you want. I'm sure that Logan won't care if you get extra, so get some different flavors."

"I don't know how much I'll be making yet." Holly nodded and started to put several of the small containers in the cart. "I

62

don't want that."

"Yes, you do. It's written all over your face. And if you put it back, I'll just buy it and bring it to your house for you. So pick out the flavors you like and we can move on." Charlie picked ten of them that were on sale, but she tried her best not to look at anything else longingly.

They ended up with two carts of items. There hadn't been any paper towels, toilet paper, or napkins at the house. Holly had called Logan three times with questions, and the last time she'd handed Charlie the phone. He was laughing and she felt her temper rise up, thinking he was laughing at her.

"I'm so glad that Holly found you and thought of those extras. We'd have been in real trouble without toilet paper. Are you having fun?" She wasn't sure what he meant and said so. "Having fun with Holly. She's funny when she's not mad at me. Which isn't as often as one might think."

"We're spending a lot of money here. I mean, lots." He told her it was fine. "No. You don't understand. We have two carts of food and things here. And now we have to go and get toilet paper and things like that."

"It's fine. I promise you. There is plenty of money on the card. In addition to working on the ranches for my family, I also do some computer work and translations for the local colleges. I have money." She was still worried. "When you get here, don't be alarmed if you see a bunch of trucks in the drive. My brothers and I are trying to locate Zach's tractor. They said that they delivered it."

"Was it delivered on a flatbed?" He told her it was. "Then look at the local car dealership. It's more than likely there. If it's

63

close to here, we can go by and see if it's there or not on the way back to your home."

"That would be fantastic. Let me know. And we have to get you a phone." She asked him why. "So I can talk to you when I need something. Unless you'd let me taste you."

Her body heated up. It was a feeling that she'd never felt before. Desire swamped her, the need to have him taste her, anywhere, made her moan. And when he said her name, soft and full of promise, she handed the phone back to Holly. Walking away, not sure what was going on with that, she went out in the evening air and took several deep breaths. Christ, that was...that was amazing, she thought.

The night air was cold, too cold really for her to be standing out in it in a borrowed flannel shirt and her tennis shoes. But it felt good on her heated body, and she could smell the freshness of it too. The air in the city, where she lived, smelled of diesel and people. Not a good combination.

Going back in the store, she wasn't surprised to see Holly talking to the cashier as she loaded things on the belt. Helping her, Charlie was grateful when she didn't ask her where she'd gone and why. However, when they were loading the truck up with her things, she asked her if she was all right.

"Yes. Just overwhelmed again." She told her about the car dealership. "If you can tell me where it is, I'll drive by to let them know."

"All right. But you're all right then?" She nodded and told her she was fine. "If you need me, just call. Logan said he was going to get you a cell phone to carry. I'll make sure that all our numbers are programmed in."

"Thanks."

As she drove back to the house, all she could think about was Logan. And when she pulled in after driving by the dealership, seeing all the trucks, she was glad there were others there. She didn't want to have to explain to him what the fuck was wrong with her. As if she had any idea herself.

CHAPTER 5

After his brothers left, happy that the tractor mystery was solved, he went to find Charlie. She was sitting on the deck with a blanket around her when he found her. Sitting down in the chair next to hers, he said nothing as they watched the dark woods behind them.

He thought about how she had panicked. Holly told him that she'd gotten this odd look on her face and nearly ran from the store. He had thought about what he'd said, how she might have taken it, and wondered how he could explain it to her. When she cleared her throat, he was going to try and talk to her if she was going in.

"When I was seventeen years old, I was a sophomore in college. I have this, I guess some people call it a photographic memory. But I can also recall with perfect clarity photographs, as well as sounds, smells, and other stimuli." He told her what he thought it was. "Yes, eidetic memory. It was like I could read or see something, and see it in my head when I needed to call up information. Same with sounds and smells. It's why I was able to do so well in school."

"Languages as well, I bet." She nodded. "I was good in school. I had three scholarships all lined up to go to college on a free ride. But that would mean that I'd have to go away, not be able to work on the ranch. And we were desperately trying our best to hang on to it then."

"Holly told me that you guys were barely making it back then." She nodded and leaned back, sure that whatever she was getting to was important to her. "Then one day, right out of the blue, I discovered that I could draw. And well. I could recall pictures I'd see. Photographs, paintings, whatever it was, I could see them. But then quite by accident, I realized that I could draw them as well. It took me nearly a year of trying to get other people's work out of my head to be able to do my own things."

He didn't interrupt her. While she'd been at the store, he'd read the file on her that Gerard had been able to find. Including her job at the advertising firm, as well as what had happened the day that her boss had shot the people she had worked with.

"I was very careful about what I did for clients. Never giving too much of myself to the drawings, but enough that they'd be happy with my work. Several times, over the course of working there, I saw works of art—my boss was a collector of them— hanging on his walls." He asked her if she knew what they were. "Yes. They were original works of art. Some of them, all of them really, had been stolen at some point, and it had been in the papers enough that all of us that worked there were speculating on how he'd gotten them. But I kept my head down, did my job, and tried not to bring any attention to myself and what I knew. Because you see, even then I was watching my pennies, trying to keep my head above water with my bills."

"You needed the money so you kept quiet. I don't blame you. I would more than likely have done the same thing." She nodded. "That day, did you know what was going to go down? That he was going to come in there with a loaded gun and shoot those people."

She didn't answer him. But Logan was a patient man; he watched the trees sway, the lights from the stars above them flicker across the pool cover, and the moon go in and out of the clouds. When she was ready, he knew, she'd tell him.

"When I called the FBI, I told them my name. I suppose that was my first mistake. Then I told them the names of the paintings, all of them that I'd seen while I was working there. I gave them the painter's name; the last place the art had been hanging, as well as the date that it was stolen. I had all they needed because I'd read about anything and everything I could put my hands on about the paintings and their history." He nodded, not liking where this was going. His heart hurt for her. "When he came into work that day, I was surprised. The agent that I had spoken to, he told me that they were going to take him into their offices to ask him about them. Little did I know, the agent decided to let him go after asking him about the paintings to see if he would lead him to the person he bought them from. Instead, he came to work."

"Christ." Logan had read the accounting of what had happened. Had read about the way the man had come in, shot everyone he could see, and then went to stand in her office. While there, he shot himself. Just put the gun under his chin and pulled the trigger.

"He knew it was me. I don't know how; the agent swears that he didn't tell him, but he knew. And when he came into my office where I was hiding under the desk, he told me what they'd told them. Mr. Ricks said that he knew that I'd turned him in, that I thought I was going to be getting a reward for turning my boss in, but he knew differently. My boss said that I was going to get nothing because they believed that I was a scorned lover and had helped him get the paintings, but now was upset with him so I turned him in."

"Do you remember the agent's name?" She just looked at him. "I'm sorry, of course you do. Tell me who he is and I'll have a friend of mine look into this."

She told him. "I had to spend all my savings to get cleared of it, and still it wasn't enough. I lost my job, my car, and my house. There was nothing left after this was finished. I can't get a job in my field because of the things that he told them. The way the entire case had been handled. I'm afraid to paint, even a color by number, for fear of someone remembering another painting and me being involved with it. Not even firms that I could work with that have nothing to do with advertising will let me in the front door."

"I'm so sorry." He was too. She'd gone through so much, and for no other reason than she'd worked for the wrong person. "Are you telling me this, Charlie, because you think it's going to make a difference on if you live here or not?"

"Yes. Your family has a good reputation. A good name around here. I might not live in this area, but I've heard of the

70

Douglas brand. I've even seen your cheese on the television." He joked about how bad the label was. "It is. You need something less cute and more serious. And with your wine to go with it, you should pair them up."

It hit him she was right. Not only should they pair them up, but he wanted to open a shop to sell homemade crackers and the family cheese. Things with cows on them for the children and their wines to the parents. When he stood up and pulled her into the house behind him, he started talking about his ideas, what he wanted to see.

"Not all the stuff needs to be serious. There should be items with cows on them in a cute way for the kids, just a section of them. I don't know what we'd put there, but I'm sure you can figure that out with me. The wine label, it needs to be serious, like you said, with grapes...No, not grapes...those have been done to death. Something with flair." He searched around until he found a pad of paper in the big desk and several pencils. After giving them to her, he began pacing as he spoke. "We're McBride and Douglas. Snow too, if you can work that in there somehow. Perhaps just the initials with something under it to explain, I don't care. And then the dairy one. They'd have to approve, of course, but we could have tags made that would hang on the items we'd sell. Wine stoppers and cutting boards. Oh, yes, I can see something on a cutting board that we could sell with the cheese. A—"

"Hang on a second." He watched her hand race over the piece of paper. He had more ideas, more things that he wanted to do. Taking the other pad, he sat down and began writing out things he wanted to do, how he had to find items he wanted. And things he wanted to look up. "How's this?"

He stared at the drawing. It was perfect. But taking it from her hands to get a closer look, he could see too that she'd gotten all the details in it that he'd wanted. The script of their initials, the stacks of wine crates in a field just under the initials. Across the bottom of the mocked up label he could see their names, Douglas, McBride, and Snow Incorporated.

"I'd suggest that you take a photograph of the vineyards and then one of the crates of grapes. Then superimpose the crates over it for a crisp look. Maybe have a few of the fruit spilling over the side." He nodded, walking around the desk where she was sitting. "I could do better than that, it's just that you were saying what you wanted too fast and I could hardly keep—"

Logan pulled her from the chair and kissed her. It was just a simple kiss, something to say to her that he loved it, her work. But when she looked up at him, her eyes bright with need, he lowered his head again and deepened the kiss, pulling her body flush with his.

Her arms went up and around his shoulders. Her body, warm and soft, pressed tighter against his. Logan wanted to ask her if this was all right, to see if he'd overstepped the bounds, but she moaned then, the hum of it seemingly a part of him. When he lifted her up, cupping her ass tightly in his hands, she wrapped her legs around him and he moaned with her.

Clearing the nearly empty desktop of everything on it by sweeping his hand across the desk, he laid her back on it. They tore at each other's clothing. Buttons went flying. His belt smacked him in the head when she jerked it off him. When her shirt was up and over her breasts, Logan filled his hand with

72

her flesh, biting her gently through the soft material that was the only thing between him and his prize. Lifting that, too, out of his way, he suckled on her nipple hard before taking her entire breast into his mouth and rocking into her.

"Please."

He lifted his head, looking down at her again, seeing her desperation, feeling much the same way. Standing up, he pulled her pants off and then his own. His cock ached to be inside of her, pre-cum dripping from him in long streams as he fisted himself. When she sat up, wrapping her hand around his as he held his cock, he cried out when she licked him. Christ, he wanted to come now.

Kissing her, pushing her body back to the desk, he slid his cock over her heat. She was wet, heated, and her lips seemed to be pulling at him. And when he fucked her, sliding his crown over and over into her, she lifted her hips up, using his thighs as leverage. Then when she cried out, her body bowing up off the desk, he slammed forward and rolled over the abyss with her.

It wasn't enough. They both, it seemed, needed so much more. Fucking her harder now, he lifted her ass up off the desk so that he could pound her deeper. He fucked her mouth with his tongue. With his free hand Logan cupped her breast, and when he could pull himself from the dark sweetness of her mouth, he'd lean down and suckle at it. She came a second then third time as he moved to the pounding pulse at her throat. The need to mark her, to taste her, had him nearly coming again. And when she dug her nails into his back, screaming that she was coming again, Logan bit down, tearing into her tender flesh as he felt her tighten around him, nearly strangling his cock.

He emptied into her three times. Each time he came, his balls would fill almost as if he had an endless supply of energy and cum. Logan cried out when she cupped his ass, bringing him as hard against her as she could get him when he came again. This time, he knew there would be no quick recovery from this. He was finished.

His body was spent, yet he wanted her again, wanted to feel her body tighten around his again while he fucked her. Logan held her to him, held her warm body to his like a favorite blanket.

When her arms dropped from him, he knew that she was finished as well. Logan lifted his head from her throat and looked down at her once again. She was beautifully sated, her body marked by his, teeth marks all over her throat and breasts. Then it hit him. Christ, he'd taken her like a mate.

~~~

Charlie woke up when she was put into a bed. Smiling, she reached for the man who had given her so much, and looked up when she heard the door shut. Logan was gone, and the light under the door in the hallway was darkened a few seconds later. Sitting up in the bed, she looked around. He'd put her to bed and left her. He'd left her.

Not sure what to do, she laid back down. He at least hadn't left her on the desk like some sort of hooker. Getting up, she went to the bathroom and left the light off. Turning on the shower, she stood there thinking about what had happened. They'd had sex, yes, and it had been amazing. And when he'd bitten her...he'd bitten her.

Putting her hand over the small scar there, she thought of all she knew about mates and bites. How sex bonded them and made them one soul. He'd bitten her then left her alone. As if he was ashamed of what he'd done.

"Now don't jump to conclusions, Charlie. He might have just gone down to lock up." Yes, she thought, and monkeys were going to take flight right out of her ass too. Getting under the spray, she let the tears fall. The first time in her life she had enjoyable sex, and the guy had hated it.

After washing her hair three times, simply because she could, she washed her body hard. Sore places were all over her; her nipples were especially tender. But ignoring the little aches and pains was better than remembering his mouth on her, his cock deep inside of her. Finishing up, she used the towel on her body like a weapon, drying her skin so roughly that she knew that she'd be sore when she was done. When she got dressed, Charlie sat in the chair that was near the open door to the upper deck. To wait for him. To talk when he returned.

He wasn't locking up, she told herself an hour later. And if he had, then she was pretty sure it wouldn't have taken this long. Not that she wanted him to sleep with her, but he'd just left her. Thinking of how she'd been treated the other two times she'd had sex, Charlie thought that if Logan would have hit her afterwards, it might have been less painful than this. Getting out of the chair, she tried to think what to do.

"I have no car nor money, so leaving isn't going to happen. Not unless I want to hitchhike back. Then where will I go? I don't have any money for that either." Her belly tightened when she thought of the man who had offered her paradise then taken it away. "It's not like you were fighting him off, Charlie. You're as much to blame for this as him. Perhaps those men were right, I am a terrible lay."

When the sun came up over the trees, she was no closer to trying to figure out what to do than she'd been before. Acting like nothing had happened might work, but she wasn't so sure. The man had put his dick inside of her, and she'd screamed out his name several times. Pulling on her shoes, she made her way to the kitchen and out of the house. Lingering over breakfast with him at this point wasn't an option.

Charlie found a man in one of the big barns. It smelled of fermenting fruit, which she supposed was about right since there was wine making going on. When she introduced herself to him and told him she was there to work, he asked her what she knew of grapes. His English was broken up, so she answered him in Italian.

"I can tell you everything you'd ever want to know about them that's in print. However, if you're asking me how much experience I have in making wine, picking them or anything else that goes on with them, then absolutely nothing." He grinned at her. "But I'm a quick learner and not afraid of hard work."

"My son, Percy, will take you out with him. Today we are cutting vines. Then we're going to start some new sets with them." She nodded and he handed her an apron, gloves, and a pair of clippers. "Watch him and he'll show you what to cut and what not to cut. When you have it down, we'll set you on a row."

Percy spoke better English, but she enjoyed talking to him in his native language. He not only showed her how to clip the tender vines, but how to figure out if what she cut was going to be used in the vineyard as a replacement. They were working so well together that she didn't realize how much time had passed until a big bell sounded.

"Lunch." Nodding, she moved toward the orchard that was on the property, which was part of the wine making, instead of the barn. She wanted to be alone and have a few of the apples. She was enjoying her second apple when a large cougar stepped in front of her.

"One of the brothers or Logan?" He laid down. "I'm guessing not Logan. I have no idea why, but I think he would have come out here on his horse and not as a cat where I can't talk to him. And I'm pretty sure that he can talk to me anyway since I tasted his blood."

Of course the cat said nothing. As she ate her last apple she looked around the place she was sitting. It was breathtakingly beautiful here. The rows and rows of grapes; the trees at the end of each of them heavy with blooms. When the cat yawned, she did as well.

"I didn't get much in the way of sleep last night. I'm sure, if the lore is right, you can smell him on me. Anyway, not much sleep. I came out here when I wasn't sure what to do with myself. I don't think he enjoyed it as much as I did." The cat lifted his head and looked at her, and she wondered if he would tell his brother what she said. "I'm using you as sort of a confessional. Which means, you can't tell anyone what I'm saying. Deal?"

He nodded and laid back down. Keeping an eye out for Percy, she picked herself a fourth apple and ate it. It wasn't as good as the first two were, but not as bad as the third one had been. She thought perhaps that the luster of picking and eating her own lunch was soured now. When the cat stood up, she looked in the direction that he was.

Logan. And he was with another man. The closer they got to her, the more she could see that whatever had happened between them hadn't affected him at all. He was his usual self…whatever that meant about him. When he was close enough to talk to her, she reached down and touched her fingers to the fur of the cat. Logan nodded to the cat.

"Zach." She looked at the cat when he stretched out and then looked up at her. There were marks around his face, small darker places there that she could use to tell the difference on him the next time. When he took off to the woods, she started back to work. "I was telling Palmer, Palmer Snow here, about the work you did last night."

"It was nothing." Both men fell in step on either side of her. She wanted them gone, but didn't want to lose her job before she got paid. "Percy is showing me how to cut the vines. I should be good enough at it soon to be left to my own row."

"I wanted to talk to you about the artwork, if you have time." She turned to Logan and said that she was working for him, so whatever he wanted. When his face turned a little red, she felt a little better about how hurt she was. "Palmer has a few ideas that he's looking for art done up on. Something to do with his line of business." She looked at the other man, the Snow of the three names on the label she'd done up.

"Whatever you need. So long as Mr. Douglas is all right with me working for you too. I was hired on to work the vineyards." She was being catty, she knew that, but she was making the point that last night was a one-time deal. "I should get back to work."

When Percy returned, she'd cut three of the vines. He told her she'd done a good job and showed her where to start on another row. When he passed her—she was much slower than him—she stood there and let the tears fall again. Charlie felt like a fool.

When he came to find her, Percy said that he was going to go home for dinner. Nodding at him, telling him she was nearly to the break, she didn't stop working when he left her there. When she was finished, she stood up and made her way back to the house. Not sure what sort of reception she was going to get, Charlie took off her shoes and left them by the door. If she was unwelcome, she'd have them ready to take.

Going into the kitchen, she found it to be empty and started pulling things from the pantry and fridge to make something for dinner. Finding two steaks in the sink, she worked around those.

Charlie wasn't going to assume that one of them was for her, so she made a heavy salad. There were plenty of things to put on it should he have company, and when she stuck it back in the fridge he stepped in the kitchen with her. Turning her back to him, she explained what she was doing.

"I have potatoes in the oven if that's okay, and I've made some green beans and a salad. Will someone be joining you?" He told her just her. "Okay then. I have a salad too. Would you like some of it?"

"I'm not much of a salad eating sort of person. But I'll have some. Charlie, I wanted to talk to you about last night." She turned to him and told him she didn't want to. "I think it's important that you understand, I never meant for that to happen. And I certainly never meant to mark you."

"I understand." He wiped his hand over his face and looked frustrated. "It's all right. We're two grown adults who had an itch. It's over, I work for you, and we're fine."

"I had a mate." She said she knew that. He'd told her. "You can't be my mate. I had my one chance at that and it's gone."

She wished now that she had taken her chances and stayed at her old apartment. Turning back to the sink, she tried to gather her hurt around her and speak in a calm and normal voice. She'd not show him how badly he was hurting her.

"I have to go into town tomorrow. I'm going to see if I can hitch a ride with one of the others." He told her she could use the truck. "No. I don't want to. I'd rather hitch a ride, and barring that, I can walk. I love walking."

They ate in silence. The only sound coming from the table was the clicking of forks against the plate and the clinking of ice in the glasses. Mostly Charlie moved her dinner around on her plate and ate very little of it. When he said he was finished, that things were delicious, she nearly snatched his plate from him to take to the sink. When someone knocked at the front door and he went to answer it, she was never so glad to be alone in her life.

Clean up was easy. After she was done she made her way to her room again and closed the door. Not sure what was going on down in the living room or if she'd be welcome, she had no desire to hang out with Logan anyway. Finding a book on one of the shelves, Charlie took it out on the deck and sat in one of the chairs there. She was going to have to do something, and soon. There wasn't any way she was going to be able to stay here and feel like this all the time.

CHAPTER 6

Logan got out of his truck at Mason's and stood by it. He had to talk to someone about this, but he didn't want to feel stupid. It had been four days since he'd made love to Charlie. Four days and five nights of torture. Every time he thought of her body, how she had screamed out his name, he felt his cock stretch. And his cat was royally pissed off at him too. He could smell her as well as he could, and they both wanted her.

When he heard a noise behind him, he looked at Susie as she came out of the barn. Her smile made him smile back, but when she stopped moving and frowned at him, he knew that she'd done some poking around.

"You're not happy." He shook his head. "Neither is your roommate, is she? I'm guessing that you've not settled this thing between you, have you?"

"She won't talk to me about it." Susie nodded and made her way to the corral where Mason had three horses. Logan followed her. "Yesterday she came up with this artwork for Palmer and he paid her. Then she did something for Zach, for his grain. I think he's having some business forms made up. Regardless, I think she's hoarding money so she can leave me. Leave here."

"Hoarding is a strange name for saving your money." He rubbed his hand over his face, as he'd done a thousand times over the last few days. "What has you so tied up in knots? The lack of sex? I'm pretty sure that if you were to go into town and state that you needed a good lay, there would be a line before you were naked."

"I don't want that." She looked at him. "It's not sex. It's that she's so.... When we have dinner together, the only meal that she comes to the house for, it's like we might as well be alone. I tried asking her about what she's learning, and I get straightforward answers that are less than friendly. More like she's reciting what she thinks I need to hear. Then after dinner she cleans up and goes to her room. I don't see her again until the following day."

"Have you tried...? Why do you have to see her before she goes out to do the job you hired her for?" He told her he had no idea. "I see. So she's doing the job that you asked her to do, cleaning up after the two of you after she cooks dinner. Charlie tells you what she does, does artwork for anyone that asks her, and is saving her money. The bitch. I think you should have the pack take her out and kill her."

She was missing the point. When she laughed, he wanted to punch something. Not her—she'd hit him back—but he was frustrated and she wasn't helping him. Looking at the house, he wondered if Mason would be any more helpful.

"He won't, you know. Mason, I mean. He'll not understand

what the hell you're so tied up for any better than you do. Have you given any consideration to the thought that she's your mate?" He told her that she was dead. "Yes, I know that Mary died when you were both children. But you might have been given another chance at love. It certainly sounds like it to me."

"We're only given one person to love." She asked him if he'd loved Mary. "I don't know what you mean. We were so young. But we both knew what we were to each other, and when she died, so did a part of me."

"I would imagine it did. And since Charlie has been in your home — and I'm saying your home because it sounds to me like she doesn't feel all that welcome there — has that part of you remained dead?" He just looked at her. "Logan, she's your mate and you're treating her like a live in maid."

"No. No, I'd never do that." She pointed out that she was getting paid to cook and clean for him. "That's not what she's doing at all. We both do part of the work."

But he'd not been doing anything. Yesterday when he'd come downstairs he'd noticed that the living room was cleaned up, dusted, and the pillows fluffed up. His laundry had been in a basket on the dryer too. He had no idea when she'd done that; he didn't figure she was in the house enough to get those things done. Even the dishes from his meals, including the ones where she didn't eat with him, were done up and put away. Logan leaned heavily against the fence.

He thought about how many times a day he thought of her. Wondered if she was eating well or getting enough rest. Twice now while in the shower, he'd thought of her naked on his desk and had come. When she was in the house, his cat would snarl at him, telling him to find her, to take her, but he'd been avoiding any contact with her, telling himself that she was nothing to them. But she was. Charlie was everything to them.

"I'm an idiot." Susie said he was, but what was he going to do about it. "Find her and…I haven't any idea what I should do. What would you do?"

"Tell her what you've been thinking about. How much you want her, need her. Tell her that you love her. You do, don't you." He nodded, his heart hurting for the way he'd been treating her. "You're lucky that she's not just left you, Logan. You've not been a very good mate to her."

"I haven't. I've been an idiot and a fool. Christ, she's been right there all along and I've never noticed it." He kissed her on the cheek and made his way to his truck. Stopping, he turned back to Susie to thank her again. "I owe you. Big time. Whatever you want, it's yours."

"I need a sister-in-law that can take you on." He grinned at her. "Flowers, Logan. Pamper her. She deserves that and more from you. You've a lot of time to make up for."

His mind was swirling around over and over about what he was going to do for her. Not to her. Yes, he wanted to make love to her. Take her to that big empty bed that he'd been tossing and turning in and make her his again. Even thinking of eating a full meal with her, with conversation and joking around with her, appealed to him. He'd been so lonely. And he knew that he had no one to blame but himself. His phone ringing made him smile. He had no idea who it might be, didn't care if it was a sales call; he was in too good a mood to let even one of those guys bother him. But when he said his name, the pause there was just long enough to make him nervous.

"Sir." The connection was static so he lifted his foot from the gas pedal. "You should come home now. There's been.... The miss, sir, she's been hurt."

"How bad?" There was more crackling on the line. Words were spoken but he couldn't make them all out. Ambulance. Blood. Knife. "I'm coming."

Then the line went dead. Reaching out to his family he told them what he knew. Zach was close he said, as his cougar, but he was on his way. Mason was next, and said he would be there in two minutes by horse. They were getting to her and he had no idea what was wrong.

Trying to reach out to her, all he got was a headache for his trouble. Twice he could feel something, a brief touch, but he'd not talked to her about speaking to each other, because it had never occurred to him to try. She wasn't his mate, he'd reasoned, so there was no need for it.

By the time he got there, the ambulance and three cruisers were there, as well as Landon and Mason. Zach was near the big barn and there were people milling about that he didn't know. When he started to where the ambulance had stopped, Landon stepped in front of him.

"I need to see her." He nodded but didn't move. "Landon, I just figured out she's my mate, and I have to see her."

"About time, boy. But you go over there now and you're going to kill her." He looked at the older man. "They're working on her, but they're not going to be able to if you get in their way, now will they? Mason told me over and over that you guys are possessive. So if you stay right here, I won't have to pay out a big bunch of money to have a new wing put on the hospital because you went a little batty. Logan, you have to trust this old man in this and stay put for her. I ain't seen her yet, but she's in good hands. Cut real bad but gonna make it, they promised me."

"You could have started with that." He said he might not have heard him. "No, probably not. What happened, do you know?"

"You're not gonna like that none better than you do that she's hurt. I should have thought of them coming back here. Never thought they'd be hurting people, but I'm not always perfect. My Katie, she'd tell you I never am, but—" Logan asked him to get to it. "I'm working the fences, boy. Just give me a damned minute. That son of William's showed up here. I know it was him by how she described him."

"Christian was here? And hurt Charlie?" Landon nodded and leaned against the truck. Logan thought about going to Charlie again, but he really was afraid of hurting the men trying to help her. "What did he want?"

"He wanted to burn you out. Not the house but the grapes. Charlie, she was working the line and saw him. Don't know much more than that, but he's laying out there in the rows next to the place where she was cut up." He asked if she'd killed him. "No, but he's not gonna be that pretty boy he used to be no more."

Landon laughed a little, then looked out over the field. Logan watched as the men around her began to stand up, and a gurney that had been nearby was being lowered and moved. He took the necessary steps to be with her, calming his cat with the promise that she was going to be theirs from now on. But as soon as he saw her, he had to stop and hang onto something. It just happened to be Mason.

"Steady there. I have you." Nodding, he let Mason take him the rest of the way to the gurney she was on. Her eyes were closed and her heartrate was a little slow, but steady. "They gave her something to put her out to work on her. She wasn't fussing at them but those boys, they were scared for her. That man over there, he cut her badly."

"What did he do to her?" He looked at Mason when he didn't answer him. "Mason, what did Christian do to her that has the medics scared?"

"He cut her arm badly. Right to the bone. There were other cuts, pretty bad ones, that they said are going to need some time to heal. But he took the knife to her belly. They're worried about those cuts." He noticed the blood then, how the sheet over her was saturated with it. "When I got her, she was holding in her belly, Logan. He eviscerated her."

Logan looked at her and felt his own belly churn up. When he looked at his brother, he noticed that he was blurry; he could hear but it was muffled and low. Then he simply blacked out as he heard Mason say, "Well fuck."

~~~

Zach sat very still while waiting with his family. He didn't want anyone to ask him questions about Charlie. He didn't want to think, not one thing, about what he'd seen when he'd found her. He couldn't close his eyes, couldn't blink without seeing her laying there, her hands holding herself together like that. He stood up when he felt the bile in his throat burn again.

"Breathe." He looked over at Mercedes when she spoke. "Just breathe in your nose and out your mouth. Do it, damn it."

Zach did as she said, never taking his eyes from hers. Zach could see her still, his friend, and Charlie had become one over the last two weeks. Tears fell down his face, his vision blurred, but he never stopped breathing like he'd been told, ordered really, and he didn't stop looking at Mercedes.

"I thought she was dead when I got there." She nodded and told him to breathe. "I've never seen anyone so hurt like that before. And she talked to me. Told me to call an ambulance in a calm voice that had me thinking that she was okay, that it wasn't as bad as I was seeing, you know? She said she thought she was hurt. She's laying there bleeding and her belly is.... She just thought she was hurt."

"She was calming you. Did she tell you not to look at her but at her face?" He nodded. "That's my girl. She was calming you down so that you could think. Did you? I bet you thought in a nice order of things you needed to do, right?"

"Christian was screaming that he was hurt too. He was about ten feet down from her. Going on and on about how it was his land, his vineyard, not some child his father hadn't even acknowledged." Zach had heard how his brother had gotten the winery, and was pretty sure that Mercedes had as well. "My cat wanted to protect her, save her, but she kept telling me to stay with her and not bother with Christian, that he wasn't worth it."

"She thought you were going to kill him." Zach said that he wanted to. "Zach, she saved you a lot of explaining. Kept you calm and steady until someone got there to help you. You all right now?"

"Yes." He was too, feeling better just talking and not thinking. "The police are gonna want to know what was said. Christian

88

admitted that he was the one that hurt her, and that he'd do it again if given the chance. He screamed about wishing it was Logan. Christ, I know this sounds terrible, but I wish it had been him and not her. She's only human."

"I do too." He looked at Logan and hugged him. Logan would make this better. Zach wasn't a baby, he was a grown man, but right now he wanted to sit in a corner and sob like a child while sucking his thumb. "Thank you for being there with her for me. She's my mate. I just…well, I had it pointed out to me this morning."

"Well, duh, dumbass." They both laughed. "You and her need to talk when she's better. I mean, really talk. She had some things in her head that are just depressing. And she worries about her mom and what is going to happen to her if you don't pay her enough. Logan, that girl has seen some shit."

"I know, and I'm going to help her in any way I can. I've hurt her. I know that. And I neglected her. My cat and I both have. It never occurred to me what she was to me. And now, it might be too late." Zach asked him what he'd heard. "That she's lost a great deal of blood, but thankfully the medics got to her before infection could get in and harm her more. While she was cut really badly, her intestine looks to be intact, and they won't have to remove any of it. But she's going to be sore, laid up for some time after this."

They sat for another three hours while she was in surgery. The nursing staff was great, coming out to give them updates when they could. Nothing changed. She was still in grave condition, but the doctor was hopeful. When Zach stood up to go outside for some fresh air, he made a call to his friend, Ed Clarke. After asking after Charlie, the man got down to business.

"I've looked into those things you asked me about. Yes, the company that you purchased the tractor from has a very good record. However, the company that they use to make deliveries is a little on the shady side." He asked him how. "Had Charlie not thought of the car dealership when she had and someone gone out there to bring the driver and his rig to your home, I think you might have been out the cost of the tractor as well as the item itself. This is a scam that they have used on several occasions."

"They drop it off there and someone comes and gets it. You know, Charlie said the same thing. She told me that when she'd gone by to check on the trailer, it wasn't sitting in a place she might have seen it had she not been really looking for it. And the dealership was surprised that it had been left there. So now what do we do?" Ed laughed and told him he was going to do nothing. "Leave it to you then? I don't think so, Ed. They were told where to deliver it and when. The fact that we had someone that thinks outside the box is the only reason that I've got it."

"I know, but I'm working with the tractor supply company now. They've gotten some pretty good lawyers on their end. I think they're hoping that with another delivery going out, they'll be able to catch not only the men who are on this end, but the receivers too." Zach liked that idea. "Now to the other. I must say, I'm very proud to be working with you on this one. It says a lot to your character as well as how you were raised, young Zachery. Your parents would be very proud of you."

"Had it not been for some very important people around when we needed them most, there is no telling what might have happened to us. Aunt Georgie stepping in when she did. You

90

being there even though we had no idea what you were doing. Palmer and the rest of them. We're only a family because of them." Ed said that he'd only done what he thought was right. "Yes, just like the good man that you are."

"Well, I've set things in motion. And at the beginning of next month, the building will go under the knife, so to speak. Once that is started, we'll work on the rest of it." Zach thanked him again. "No, thank you. I'm enjoying this more than I can say."

He'd purchased the building from the city for a buck. Not even Emma, the mayor, knew who owned it yet, as he'd worked with Ed and had it under a corporation that was simply called Childlike. And when it was finished, he planned to use it as a home for children and their families who came out to see the ranch that Susie and Gerard ran.

There would be three floors when it was complete, with four bedrooms on each level, along with a living room, kitchen, and a medical room. Right now he was working with the hospital to see what would be needed as an emergency facility for the family to use, as well as a nurse per family while they were there.

There would be a stocked kitchen, staff to cook and clean up after them, and also an entertainment center that would carry games, movies, as well as other things both children and adults could use. The lower level was for parking for the family, as well as a small restaurant in the event they needed a night out.

He was still standing there when his brother told him that Charlie was out of surgery. But before he could make his way in, Ed called him again. This time all joking was put off, and he told him about what he'd just found out from the place he'd gotten his tractor from.

"They've lost nine shipments over the last several months. Not only larger pieces of equipment such as yours, but also truckloads of smaller items such as snow removal items, salt, as well as feed for animals. Just last spring they had an entire shipment of chicks go missing." Zach asked if it was from the same place. "You mean out of the same warehouse? No. They have several across the United States that they use for different products. It wasn't until I made inquiries on it that they started looking deeper into it and asking questions of their distribution centers across the country."

"Why didn't they look?" Ed told him what the company told him. "So they expect a little loss. But this seems like just a bit more than little. Truckloads aren't something to just roll under the rug. And I know how much I paid for that tractor, so how many times can they be hit with that coming up missing before they start to think that something is fucked up?"

"Your tractor would have been the third missing in a year. Yes, it's costly, but if the company isn't being made aware of it, or someone doesn't check the paperwork coming from these places, then why would they go looking for trouble?" Zach said that was just stupid. "Yes. Reminds me of the things that were going on in our own little town. If Holly hadn't started looking into things, there is no telling how much longer this might have gone on. More than likely until we were bled dry."

They made plans to talk later in the week at his office. Ed was a good man, and now that he had someone helping him out, he was less stressed too. As Zach made his way back into the hospital, he moved to listen to what the doctor was telling them.

"She's strong, young, and in good shape. All things that are

92

helping her come out on the good end of this. Charlie will need to rest a great deal, relax and not work at all. I don't want her even lifting a loaf of bread. She had some serious injuries. Is there someone that can care for her when she leaves here?" Every one of them raised their hands. "I see. Well, she's going to need you all. Not only will she have to change her diet for a little while, but she'll need to not lift, as I said, be careful she doesn't tire too much, as well as a great many other things I'm sure that right now I'm not thinking of."

"We'll make sure that she stays put." Zach wouldn't want to be Logan when he tried to make her do anything. But then, perhaps she'd do well knowing that he loved her. Or maybe not. She was very stubborn, Zach had come to realize. And she thought that she wasn't worthy. That had taken him by complete surprise when she'd told him.

Zach thought that she was fast becoming his best friend and the one person in the world he could easily talk to. But he also knew enough about her to know that she was smart, but didn't realize it; tender hearted, though she tried to hide it; and that she loved Logan.

CHAPTER 7

Logan stretched out in the chair again. He was too tall, too long legged, and too tired to try and make it work anymore. Standing up, he stretched his body, hearing all the places that ached crack and pop. When he bent at the waist to touch his toes, just to get the blood flowing again, he felt his back muscles move like they had been unused for a long time.

"Why are you here?" He looked at the bed, not saying a word until she spoke again. Over the last several days she would say the strangest things, then just lay there. "Go home and leave me alone."

"I'm not touching you." Standing up, he looked at her to see if she was having another dream. "Do you know who you are?"

"Charlie Stone. You're Logan Douglas, the bane of my life." He smiled at her. "I hurt. Every.... That other man. I think I might have hurt him too."

"You did. He's in the hospital under lock and key." She

nodded and closed her eyes. "Are you going to go back to sleep again or can you talk to me a bit?"

"I don't know. I feel very strange. Like I've been having sex a great deal and this is the afterglow. But I still hurt." He sat down and took her hand in his. "He hurt me badly. I don't know what he was talking about, but I think his noodle isn't quite done yet."

Logan laughed. It felt strange after so long to do it, too. Kissing the back of her hand, he watched her eyes drift closed as he sat there. The meds she was getting were there to keep her out of pain, but to help her rest easily too. When her fingers tightened around his, he asked her if she was all right.

"I was thinking I should move out." He asked her why she'd do that. "Well, because people who work for someone shouldn't be having the kinds of thoughts about their landlord that... Logan, I hurt."

"I know, baby. I'm so sorry." Wiping away the tears, he kissed her forehead and pushed the button on her bed to call the nurse. As soon as he told her that Charlie was in pain and needed something for it, she came right in. In minutes, he could see that she'd drifted off again.

She'd been waking up like this for a few minutes at a time over the last few days. Mostly she'd say things that made no sense to him, but there were times when she was lucid enough that he could ask her about what had happened out in the fields. The police had asked him to write everything she told him down, but he wasn't sure it was very useful.

"You'd be surprised at what we're getting from her." Howie had come by to see how she was doing and to pick up some of the notes yesterday. "We know that his sister was around...Charlie saw her. And we know that he brought the knife that he used to hurt her with him. That makes it premeditated, even though Charlie wasn't the intended victim. Of course he wasn't looking for her but you, but it makes no difference to the outcome. Someone was hurt because of the two of them."

When the door opened behind him, he stood up again. He didn't want to leave Charlie, but he did need a little fresh air. His cat did as well. The smells of the hospital, the medicine, as well as the people were a little too much for long periods of time. He hugged Katie McBride when she came in.

"I was in town and thought I'd come by and bring you something to eat. I hope that's all right." He told her it was perfect. "I got the urge to bake a cake, and had to run Landon off or he'd have eaten the whole thing himself."

"He does have a very sweet tooth." He ate the thick slice of cake while she walked around the room fussing with things. "Is everything all right? I mean, you're loving that little girl, I bet."

"Oh my, yes. She's beautiful. And when I hold her, it seems to make things peaceful for me. I've not been doing well for a bit, I think." He knew that she was depressed and was seeing someone about it. Logan wasn't sure any of them were going to ever get over Dirk and what he'd done to Katie and Landon. "I'd like to ask you a favor. It's about Charlie and you."

"You know that she and I would do anything in the world for you." She nodded and brushed the hair from Charlie's eyes. "They just gave her something for pain. She was saying to me earlier how she wanted to move out."

"You won't let her, will you? She's such a lovely girl. And I know that you and she will be happy together, once you get this all behind you. I was wondering, however, why didn't you convert her? I mean, she was in the same way that my Emma was, correct? She might not have felt it with all the meds in her." When Katie sat down and held his hand, he kissed it and told her that he loved her. "Thank you, Logan. You have no idea how good that makes me feel. You're so special to Landon."

"You both are to me as well. But about converting Charlie. We thought about it, but she had lost so much blood by the time we got to her that it would have killed her had we tried. Not to mention, even shifting in the condition she was in, Aunt Georgie wasn't sure that her cat wouldn't have been in the same trouble. And had she been, then there would have been no shifting back for her. They both would have died."

"Oh, I don't think I thought of that. Poor girl. If William were alive now, he'd be so hurt by this." Logan thought that Katie was hurt too by it, thinking of her own son doing something like this. "Anyway, my favor. You know that Mason and Emma got married quickly. Why, it was done and over within minutes. No planning or anything. I want to have a big wedding, Logan. One that I can plan and organize. See someone wearing a big beautiful gown and have cake that people will talk about for years to come. A photographer that will take more pictures than you'd look at in a month. I need that."

He laughed. Logan couldn't help it, he laughed. And when Charlie looked at him then fell back to sleep, he just shook his head and kissed Katie's cheek. He dearly loved this woman.

"Would you give me a chance to ask her first? I mean to marry me. Then this whole wedding thing, you're going to talk to her about your plans. I haven't any idea if she'll go for it, but you're going to do the convincing." Katie smiled, a huge smile that lit up her face and eyes. "You have already started planning, haven't you?"

"I had to do something. What with Landon underfoot all the time now and living in a home that while I love it, it isn't mine, I need something to do." He asked her if she wanted to move out. "I think we're going to find us a small place, somewhere we can just call our own. I love living with them, they're the sweetest people in the world, and I love Mason like my own…I dearly love him, but we need our own space too. I would like a garden full of flowers I can play in. Someplace I can take my granddaughter and we can bake cookies and have crafts. Not a big place, but big enough for grandchildren to come and stay with us, without the watchful eye of their parents."

"Have you talked to your daughter?" She said not yet. "I see. Well, you know that I'd support you in anything you do. Even the wedding. But that will be up to you and Charlie. And you know that it's going to be a little while. She has some healing to do."

"I know, poor little thing. To think that that man had gone out there to purposely hurt someone. What is this world coming to?" He said he had no idea.

Logan finished off his sandwich outside in the sunshine. There were picnic tables set up in a smallish park, and it felt good to get out of the hospital for a little while. Sitting there with the sun on his face, he thought of the changes he was making in his life. And the adjustments he was making in himself too. That had been a lot easier than he'd thought it would be.

He'd been in a rut, he knew that, and he was pretty sure

that even his brothers knew it. They had branched out—even Zach had gone in a different direction in his life—yet Logan had stayed still, not bothering to see where life could take him but continuing to work at the same job at the same place like nothing had changed. But it had.

When all of them had started going their own way, he'd stubbornly stayed in the family home, nearly getting himself killed in the process because he was still living in the past. He didn't have a new truck, though he could well afford one. His boots were the ones he'd gotten when he'd graduated from high school, and he'd had them patched so many times there was more new material than original.

Every Tuesday night like clockwork he went to the diner, because that was what he'd done for years. Eating the same meal, the same way every time. They didn't even ask him what he wanted or bring him a menu anymore; they knew he wasn't going to alter his choice. He'd not even noticed it until his brother wanted to come over and said it was Tuesday, he knew he was going to the diner.

That was when Logan noticed a lot of things. After Charlie had put things away when she'd come from the store again, he found himself redoing the food, putting things in the proper place. He was standing there with a gallon of milk, a head of lettuce, and butter in his hands when it hit him. Shoving it all back in, he'd gone around the house looking at other similar anal things he'd done. His shirts were in the closet in the same order. His socks were folded, not rolled. Even his fucking fridge was the same.

When he was finished with his sandwich, he wadded up his

paper bag, tossed it in the trash without folding it, and walked into the hospital again. He was really proud that today was the first time he'd not gone back and fixed it.

~~~

Roseanna Martin waited until she could go back and see her brother. She'd been there for nearly an hour now, and no one had helped her despite them telling her that they'd be right back with her. Looking down at her legs, she pulled her skirt down more to cover up the bandage that she'd put on when she'd been hurt. Roseanna had never thought that she'd be hurt this badly for just trying to take back what was rightfully hers and her brother's.

"Ms. Martin?" She looked up at the nurse or whatever he was and smiled. "I'm sorry about the delay in taking you back. Christian is having some—"

"Mr. Martin to you." The man, Meszaros his name badge said, looked confused. "You're not in the same station in life as he is, so you'll refrain from calling him by his first name. Mr. Martin. Like I'm Ms. Martin. Now, I'd like to go back and see him. I'm all he has in the world now."

The man looked confused again, but then she could see his temper rising, the way he stood straighter and his back became ramrod stiff. Before she could remind him how much better she was than him, how she was rich and he was nothing more than a nurse, a nurse because he'd been too stupid to be anything else, he blasted her with his own words.

"Well, Miss high and mighty, you can't go back and see him because he's having some troubles passing gas. Once he farts, which is what we underlings call it, you can go back. Unless of course you'd like to go back and assist him in this." Roseanna started to stand—it was her intention to put this man in his place—but he stood taller now and she sat still. "If you address me or my staff in that manner again, I will bar you from coming up on this floor until he's taken off to prison where he belongs."

He wasn't going to go to prison, Roseanna wanted to tell him. She and Christian had had a plan; to go there, talk to the upstart that had taken their land and money, and make him see reason. If he didn't then they were well within their rights, as far as they were concerned, to have him killed. That woman, whoever she was, should have just died out there. Why she got in their way was beyond her. But she'd find out, that was for sure.

When the nurse walked away, she wondered how many people had heard him talking to her that way, and was curious why none of them had come to assist her. Or at the very least, kicked him in the head a few times. Creatures like him should know better than to even speak to people like her.

The police were everywhere on this floor. Roseanna had thought that they'd be down on the first level, where the dirty people were, but had been surprised to see about a dozen of them not just lingering in the halls, but leaning against the desk where the other nurses were, as well as at the elevators.

When she'd come up to this floor to see her brother, she'd been subjected to scrutiny by three people who obviously had gotten their clothing as a discount store, and had no style sense at all when it came to their hair. One of them didn't even have any make-up on. Disgusting. But they had demanded that she let them look through her purse, of all things, then had handed her gun over to one of the police. She told them she'd get it back or there would be hell to pay.

Standing up, her leg bothering her again, she moved along the hallway toward where she thought Christian was. Roseanna was careful not to touch anything. For a hospital, she thought that it could have used a very good cleaning, and most certainly someone should open a window. The air in this part of the hospital was stifling.

Standing outside the room number she'd been given downstairs, she could hear Christian. He was in pain, and whoever was with him wasn't helping him. Opening the door, she heard the most horrific noise before her brother started crying. She might have gone to his aid but the smell, the most nauseous smell she'd ever had the displeasure of smelling, hit her.

"Oh no. Someone get that animal out of here." The nurse that had insulted her, as well as another person in the same kind of uniform, turned to look at her. "Can you not smell that? You can't expect him to get well with odors like that coming from here."

"It was him, your brother." She looked at Meszaros, then at her brother. No, that couldn't be right, could it? "He farted, like I told you he had to do when I told you to sit tight and wait for someone to come and get you. So now you know what a rich fart smells like. Just like everybody else's."

The other nurse giggled and they helped Christian into his bed. He was still crying, sobbing really, about how he hurt. When they were gone, she went to the window to open it to get some fresh air in.

"It's stuck. Christian, call the desk and tell them to come here and open this. You shouldn't have to be in here with that smell. What did they do? Spray something? I wouldn't put it past them. That male nurse, he called me high and mighty before he—"

"Did you hear, Roseanna? They're going to take me to prison." She assured him they were not. "I don't know, Roseanna. They won't listen to me when I tell them that this woman wouldn't have been hurt if she'd not gotten in my way. Some people think they have all the rights. And then she had the nerve to hurt me. Why? I did nothing to her that you wouldn't have done if you had been closer to her."

"I was hurt too, you know. I've had to see a doctor twice now when all I wanted to do was meet with those land brokers. What is up with that now, do you know?" He told her he'd been in too much pain to deal with much. "I'll take care of it then, like I have to do everything else. And what is that stench?"

Picking up the phone for him, she told the person that answered she needed someone to come down to repair the window. Then she hung up. People were forever trying to explain why this or that couldn't be done. Roseanna didn't care. She wanted doers, not complainers.

"I've talked to the family attorney. He said that while he is saddened that we've been put out from our home, that Mother and Father could do what they wanted with their money. I fired him on the spot." She paced the room trying to get away from the stench. "He also advised that we get you a good criminal attorney, and I told him that you'd done nothing criminal so there was no need for that."

"The police came in here a bit ago and asked me all sort of personal questions. I, of course, didn't answer any of them. The nerve of some people."

The door opened and Roseanna told them to come and open the window.

"The window doesn't open. You do realize that you're on the tenth floor?" She rolled her eyes at the nurse and asked her to find someone that could manage a simple window. "They've never opened. They were never meant to. I'm sorry."

"Sorry does not open this window. I would like for you to find me your boss. Surely he has whatever someone needs to open them. I don't even care if its wide open, just enough to freshen the room a bit." The woman stood there staring at her. "What are you waiting for? Either open the window or find me someone that can."

When the nurse left them, she turned to Christian. "You should have been here this morning, Roseanna. I asked for poached eggs done medium and rye toast, and they told me I could have scrambled or fried. Do you think they're so podunk that they've never heard of poached before? And for lunch they told me that the doctor has changed my menu to high fiber until I can have a bowel movement. What a horrible thing to say to me."

"I was in the lobby just a bit ago and overheard them talking about someone that was making outrageous demands on the staff. That person is more than likely making it so you can't get the service that you deserve, Christian. I shall complain to the owner when you're released." The door opened again and she wanted to tell them that she was talking, but a man in a suit came in and cleared his throat. When she saw his name badge, she thought she might be getting somewhere now. "I want this window opened now. There is a horrific smell in here, and while it has dissipated some, I think my brother would benefit from some fresh air."

"Those windows don't open, miss. They're only there to let

in the light and show a view." Roseanna looked at the parking lot and the street below them. Not much of a view if you asked her. "There isn't any way whatsoever to get those windows open."

"Don't you have a key or something to use?" He asked her for what. "For the windows to be opened. Are you not listening to me? I have said several times now, and politely, that I need this window opened. Just do whatever you have to do to get that done. I swear to Christ; it's like talking to the fucking wall. Open this window."

When he left them, just walking out of the door, she turned to her brother again. He was in pain, she could see that now, and the stress of these people not doing as they wanted was making it worse. Holding his hand, she nearly screamed when the door was slammed back and two officers came in with them.

"You need to step away from the prisoner. You're not even supposed to be in this room without an officer with you." Roseanna looked around for this prisoner and then back at the officer. "Ma'am, you need to step back from the bed and our prisoner or I'll have to have you removed from the room."

"You most certainly will not. I don't know who you think you're speaking to like that, but this is my brother and I'm going to give him comfort." The officer moved toward her with his hand on his gun. "You need to get out of here. I haven't any idea what you think you're doing, but I will call the governor of this fine state and have him fire you."

When he put his hand on hers, the one she was holding Christian's hand with, she jerked from him. Telling him to get away from her, she screamed when he jerked her from her brother. Before she could hit him, teach him a lesson in touching her person when she hadn't allowed it, he had her on the floor and her face pressed tightly against the dirty tile.

They were reading her rights to her, as if she'd done something wrong to warrant such behavior from them. She'd not even gotten to hit either of them and they were acting like she'd pulled a gun on them. The bastards. As she was being dragged from Christian's room, she noticed that his hand, opposite from the one she'd been holding, was cuffed. And so was his leg.

"Get those things off him right now. What is this, some sort of torture encampment? He's done nothing at all wrong and you're treating him like he's some sort of monster. Let me go, damn it. Where are you taking me?" She was being taken to the elevator when she saw someone that she thought she knew. "Mr. McBride, you have to help me now. These fools are treating me like I'm subhuman. And they have Christian in leg irons. You were friends with my parents, tell them that they need to let us go. We're not to be treated this way and you know it."

"You mean like a criminal? Well, I'd say they got that about right, wouldn't you?" She asked him what he was talking about. "You and that brother of yours, you hurt one of my friends, and I'm not thinking too kindly of you right now. And that poor father of yours. How could you do that to your mother too?"

"Mother? Oh for heaven's sake. She was old and set in her ways. I have a life and so does Christian. We don't have time to play nursemaid to someone that more than likely wets the bed and has to be fed like a child." He said it was her mother. "So? Is that supposed to make me all tender toward her? It doesn't. Putting her in that home was the best thing that could have happened to her and to us. We cannot be expected to care for her

107

after what Daddy did to us in the land deal."

"She's dead." That caused her to pause; she told him that she'd not known. "You didn't know that your own mother had passed away? Good Lord, Roseanna, she's been gone for over three weeks now. Nearly a whole month."

"Well, I'm guessing that will be one less thing we'll have to worry about when Christian and I get out of here. Not that we did much anyway, but this is better in the long run. Now, will you do as I told you?" He just stood there, looking like some kind of cow poke. "Well? Are you going to tell them to let me go? I want to see my brother."

"No. I'm not going to help you at all. You've made your bed; you'll have to figure out how to lie in it."

Roseanna could not believe that he was treating her this way. And after all the good things her father had said about the man and his money. Well, she'd show them when she was finished here. She'd make sure that buyers knew his sheep, or whatever it was he grew, were a terror to people.

CHAPTER 8

Charlie knew that she was in the hospital, but how long she'd been there was fuzzy. It had been a while, she thought. She had woken up a few times, known someone was in the room with her but couldn't really see them well. A couple of times she was asked questions; nothing she could remember now, but there had been cops too.

Also, her body didn't hurt nearly as bad as it had when the ambulances had gotten to her at the vineyard. And she figured that it was because she was getting better or they were still keeping her drugged up that she didn't hurt as much. Moving her head, the only part of her that didn't scream out at her when she moved, she looked around the room. Hospital rooms had gotten a lot nicer since she'd been a kid. And this was far superior to the nursing home she'd been working in.

There was a nice couch, a big screened television, as well as dressers and pretty flowers everywhere. Of course she could see the medical supplies that went with having an ill person in the room, such as IV holders, blood pressure cuffs, and a large computer that sat in the corner. Turning when she heard something move, she looked at Logan.

Who would have thought that someone sleeping would be so sexy? He had his hat on still; it was tilted forward on his head and covered his eyes. His long arms laid over his lap loosely, like he had not a care in the world. His long legs were stretched out in front of him, and she could see that his boots were new. Wondering, not for the first time, about his inclination to wear flannel shirts all the time, Charlie smiled when she thought of the one that she'd taken from his laundry hamper and wore to bed nightly.

"You done looking?" Her face heated up when he lifted his hat from his face and smiled at her. "You seemed to be enjoying the view, so I thought I'd just let you have a look-see. Oh, and since I've taken your blood into my body—sexy, by the way, that you wear my shirts—I can read your thoughts. Do you want a couple more of my shirts to sleep in while you're here? I can surely do that for you. But, I'd like it better if you slept in the raw like I do when we get home."

"You.... I don't know what you're talking about. What are you doing here anyway? Don't you have a ranch to run?" He stood up and she swallowed three times hard, just thinking of the one other time that he'd stood over her like this. When he moaned, she felt her body heat up. "You need to go away."

"No, I like where I am just fine. And our ranch is in very good hands." He moved closer to the bed and her. "You sure are full of spit, aren't you? Can I kiss you, Charlie? It's about all I've thought of since I've been watching you."

"Why would you want to do that?" He was too close to her again. "Look, I want you to back away from me. I'm not in good shape right now, so I have no way of giving you sex again."

"Giving me sex? Okay, I deserve that. But I think you enjoyed that as much as I did, didn't you?" She was nodding before she could think that a fib might serve her better. "I've been so worried about you, love. They said that you were going to be all right, but I can only see you covered in blood and crying."

"That man, he hurt me." He sat down again, but pulled the chair closer to the bed and took her hand. "He said he wanted you, that you had stolen his land. I hadn't any idea what he was talking about, but then he started slashing at the grape vines that I'd just spent a week working on to make them perfect."

"You got in a few licks of your own, I'm happy to say." She laid back on the bed, exhausted again. "The doctor said it would be a little while until you were stronger. You lost a lot of blood, and you have some pretty extensive wounds to heal up too."

"He cut me. I thought I was going to die." When he kissed the back of her hand, she curled her fingers into his. "Zach was there. His cougar is very pretty, by the way. But he never left me. I thought he was, he was.... He looked at me when I was hurt, and I think it bothered him."

"Yes, it did. He told me later that he hurt for you and wanted to kill Christian. I'm glad you kept him steady. He might be in jail right now had you not." She said he was her friend. "He said that too. That you and him had become really close over the last few weeks."

"I *like* him." Logan laughed when her face heated up. "I like

111

you as well. Not as much as him, but you're not too bad."

"Thank you, I think. But I'd like to talk to you about that. Your liking me and my feeling the way I do about you." She didn't want to hear it, not today, and told him that. "I love you, Charlie."

"No. No, that can't be right. You said you had your mate, and I know enough about your kind to know that you only love once." He nodded. "Then you can't love me. I mean, it's all right that we're friends and sharing the work around the place and all, but you don't have to make proclamations that you don't feel. I'm fine with the way things are." He asked her if she loved him. "Logan, what does it matter what one of us feels for the other? Like I said, we're getting the job done and that's all that really matters."

"But it matters to me that you understand that I love you. And that you're my mate. It took me some time to figure that out. Apparently a hell of a lot longer than it did everyone around us, including the humans, who knew from the start. I know now, and I'm sorry for the way I've been treating you. But I'm thrilled to have you in my heart." She shook her head and had to be careful when it caused her pain. "When we get home, I'm going to show you just how much I love you every single day. I don't want you to ever feel that I'm just okay again."

She didn't say anything. Charlie wasn't sure what to say to him if she was honest. He was good looking, friendly when things went his way, and he seemed to have a good head on his shoulders. All the things her mother would have—

"My mom. Oh my God, I have to get some money to the place where she's staying. I should have.... How long have I been here?" He told her. "Oh no. They were very specific that I kept up with the payments they set.... They're going to put her in some government housing place and she'll not get the —"

"I took care of it for you. I had Ed find out where she's at and we took care of it. Also, we had to have him take over as her power of attorney, in a temporary capacity, so that he could get her bills paid and her other necessities taken care of." Charlie felt the tears fill her eyes because he'd gone to so much trouble for her. "She also has an around-the-clock nurse. There was an incident a couple of days ago that wouldn't have happened had she had better care. She's all right, but her arm has been broken and the home is going to be a great deal more careful with her from now on. They were rolling her on the bed and one of the aides dropped her."

"Oh, my poor mom. But the nursing home, what did you do to them?" He told her that it hadn't been him but Emma. "Oh my, I bet...I've seen her upset once since I've been here. She can hold her own, but when she wants something done, she certainly doesn't beat around the bush, does she?"

"No, she doesn't. Also, I hope this doesn't upset you, but I let your dad know where you are. He is a nice man." She said he was a very nice man. "I told him that as soon as you could, you and I would go up and see him. He said he'd like that very much."

"You've been very busy, haven't you? What else have you been up to?" His face turned beet red and she had to smile. "Do I want to know? Am I going to be pissed off?"

"More than likely some. First, I have to ask you something." She nodded. "Will you marry me? As soon as you're well enough

113

to walk down the aisle."

"Excuse me? Marry you? I thought we just established that we're not that good of friends." She laughed and hoped that he would join her. "You're not kidding, are you?"

"No. But I'd very much like it if you heard me out. There are a great number of things that I've done wrong concerning you. Most of which, I didn't take care of you. I know nothing about you other than the few things that your father was able to tell me. Also, Christian hurt you because of me. I hurt for that." She told him that it wasn't his fault. "No, not directly, but I still feel just horrible that you were injured and almost died. Which brings me to another thing that I've not given you. A way to contact me."

"I don't know what I'd do with a phone, Logan. I have no friends other than your family. I wouldn't order a pizza with it as I don't have any money. Not to mention, the one person that I would call has no way of answering, as he's in prison." He nodded and kissed the back of her hand again. "I just want things to go on the way that they were before."

"But they can't, love. Because before this, you were just a woman that lived in my home. Now...well, now you're my everything. As stupid as that sounds, it's the truth." She felt a slight pressure behind her eyes and then he spoke to her. *We can talk this way, anytime you need me. I should have thought of it sooner, or at the very least made it so that you could call out to me. I don't know what might have happened had Percy not been there when you needed him.*

"We can talk. Like this." He nodded, even though it wasn't a question. "Look, Logan. I think that we've gotten off on the wrong foot here. I just needed to find a job and work for some cash."

"We did get off on the wrong foot, and it was all my fault. And I'm going to change it." Charlie wanted to tell him it wasn't necessary, that things were just fine the way they were, but she looked at him, sitting there with his heart out for her to bruise or take into her own. "Charlie, will you marry me? Please? Be my wife, my love, the center of my world?"

When the door opened behind him, she looked at the woman standing there. While she'd seen her before, Charlie didn't have any idea what her name was. But when she came at her bed like she was going to harm her, Charlie tried to curl away from her when Logan covered her with his big, warm body.

~~~

Logan held onto Charlie's hand while he talked to the police. Holding her like he was, he was pretty sure that he'd not shift. It had been close there for a bit, but he was calmer now; not completely, but better than he'd been a half hour ago. That woman had come in here with the intention of harming his mate, and his cat had wanted blood.

"They're going to take her back to jail now. As it stands right now, we have her on attempted murder. When she was released three days ago, she was warned to stay away from you. Are you sure you're all right?" He nodded at the man in front of him. The young cop was human, so he didn't tell him that he'd shift and be as good as new. "Anyhoo. We're taking her to jail. I'm betting that the staff here will be glad to get her out of their hair too. She and that brother of hers are a pain in the bottom."

"Her brother tried to kill my wife a week ago." The cop nodded and wrote in his book again. Logan wanted to tell him

115

he needed to make eye contact with people to give them the impression that he was concerned, but Charlie squeezed his hand hard and he let it go. "What is going to happen to her now that you have the information that she was there as well during the attempt on my wife?"

"I don't know." Logan looked at Charlie when she laughed. "They should be able to hold her. I'm thinking she won't get bail. What do you think?"

It was on the tip of his tongue to tell him that he'd better fucking know, but Howie entered the room and asked what had been done. While the dumbass cop updated him, Logan sat back down and held onto Charlie.

I'm going to kill him. She told him he wasn't going to do any such thing. *He's not very good at this job. He has no people skills, nor does he have a clue as to what he's supposed to be doing. That alone is enough for me to want to kill him. Then there is the added fact that I'm annoyed as hell and am out for blood.*

Annoyed. Yes, I guess that's a good start on it. But the rest? It's all true. But if you lash out at him right now he's not going to help us at all. He's our only information at the moment. He nodded and laid his head on her legs. *Logan, do you think you can take me out of here? I don't mean because of the woman, the Martin woman, but I can't be here anymore. I want to feel the wind on my face and smell something that doesn't smell like antiseptic, and eat food with taste.*

I'll talk to your doctor. You'll be safer at home too, I think. At least there won't be any would-be-killers coming in with a knife. I wonder how she got that in here anyway. Charlie said it was ceramic so it might not have been caught on the x-rays at the doors. *I suppose not. But it was really sharp.* He touched the cut on his face and was glad that it had finally stopped bleeding.

Christ, that had been terrifying. She'd meant both their deaths, his and Charlie's, and for what? A few acres of land? He wasn't sure anything other than a family member was worth killing over.

"You okay?" He looked up at Howie and nodded. "I've sent him away, the cop. I'm guessing that he was going to be next on your shit list. I swear to you, Logan, I think they get younger all the time. Not to mention stupider."

"He needs better people skills, mostly in making eye contact. Also, it would be a lot more reassuring if he didn't tell them he didn't know what was going to happen to the perpetrator." Howie just shook his head and Logan laughed. It felt pretty good, all things considered. "She was going to kill her. Then when I took her to the floor, she kept screaming about how I was an upstart and that the land was hers and her brother's to do with as they wanted. I think she was trying to get us out of the way so that her brother could be set free too. I'm not sure how she came up with that idea, but she did tell us that if we'd just let her kill us, she and her brother would be happy."

"There are all kinds all over. When I just spoke to her in the cruiser before they took her away, she told me that this was all your fault that she'd had to try and kill you. And that she wasn't going to stop either. I asked her what she thought telling me was going to do for her, and she said that when you came up dead, not if but when you did, then she wanted me to know it was your fault, not anyone else's." Logan was speechless and just shook his head. "Yeah, well, if you turn up dead because of this bitch, I'm going to be very disappointed in you."

"I will be too, and I don't plan on it." Logan looked at Charlie when her hand slipped from his. She was asleep again. The nurse had given her something for pain after she'd been hurt when Roseanna had flown at them. He'd tried to keep her safe, but he'd accidently hurt her himself. "I asked her to marry me today. I don't think she has it in her head that we're going to be a good pair."

"Perhaps if she gets to feeling better and you pamper her a bit, she'll say yes. But I have some more news for you. Someone broke into your home today. Percy Jingles was there and called us before this person could do some real damage, but they managed to smash your living room and kitchen all to hell. I think you're going to need to do some renovating now." Logan looked at Charlie, wondering if she'd be safer at their home or here now. But he'd made her a promise and he aimed to keep it. "Logan, I'd like to suggest that the two of you get out of here. While I don't think they're smart enough to hire someone to come in here and try again, I can't help but think they might try if given enough time."

"Charlie wants to go home anyway. And I think with all of us, we can keep her safe and help her get up and about. The nurse that was in here earlier told us that they were going to get her up and moving soon. I can't believe it, but she said that it would help her heal to be moving." Howie told him that sounded about right. "I'm in love with her, Howie."

"You just figuring that out?" He nodded. "Never thought of you as slow, Logan. Did she have to point it out to you or did you get there all on your own?"

"My own. Slowly, but I got there." He looked over at her.

"I'm going to talk to the doctor about letting her go now. I can hire someone to come in and help out, but I can't leave her here. I think you might be right on the Martin children. I wonder why their father didn't leave anything to them. Could it be that he got them out of enough scrapes as kids and figured that he'd had enough?"

"Sound familiar? At least with the Martins, their children can't hurt them anymore. I can still see Landon lying there all beaten to shit." So could Logan. "All right. I have some things I have to get done today. You call me if you want us to come and escort you out of here. I would take advantage of it if I were you. These people are nuts."

He agreed. After Howie left, his aunt and Palmer showed up and sat with him for a little while. Then Palmer stepped into the hall to make a few calls. He told his aunt about what was going on with the Martin kids.

"That Roseanna was always one of those girls that had to be the best. And if she wasn't the best at whatever for some reason, either she wasn't talented enough or just didn't have what it took, she would pull the better person down until they were in tears or just walked away. I think that happened more often than not." Logan told her what she'd said to Howie. "Sounds like her. But I remember this about her too. She's extremely protective of her brother. Christian was sort of a wimpy child. She didn't help things by stepping in when things got over his head or he was in trouble. Had he been able to fail, I think he might have turned out all right. But now, after all this time, I think they're a lost cause."

"Do you know why the Martins didn't leave the winery to their kids? I mean, they're bad, yes, but I have a feeling that it's

119

more than just that." Aunt Georgie nodded and got up to get herself a glass of water from the pitcher that was constantly filled for him. "It's bad, isn't it?"

"Yes. At least I think so. About the time that Roseanna turned fifteen, there was this scandal at the private school where she went. I was helping out Dolly around the house for some extra money, and was at the house when the police arrived with young Roseanna in tow. Apparently she wasn't happy with her grades at school and had beaten the poor principal with a baseball bat. I mean, she nearly killed her, it was so bad." Logan said nothing, but knew that whatever had happened wasn't something that he'd ever heard of. "The police had brought her home, you see, to have her parents pay the damages, as well as Roseanna being put under house arrest. I guess because William and Dolly had donated a great deal of money to the school, they decided not to press charges. It was the stupidest decision they'd ever made, Dolly told me later."

"How long was she under house arrest?" Aunt Georgie's face reddened and he wondered what had happened. "She was let go."

"Yes. Not by the Martins, but by the police. It came out later that she'd been...Roseanna had taken it upon herself to get something on the then sheriff so that he'd leave her alone or else." He asked her if it was sex. "Yes. She would go to the office of whoever she or Christian was having trouble with, record them doing unspeakable things to her body, then blackmail them. It wasn't until about the time that William got sick that he heard about it. I think it broke his heart more than he could ever say. And Christian wasn't any better. He and Roseanna pulled all

120

sorts of scams like that, and never had even a slap on the wrist."

"And so William finds out about it, basically disowns them both, and leaves it all to me because of the daughter he had during an affair." Aunt Georgie nodded. "Then they shove their mom into a nursing home, where she was killed by a greedy bastard; again because of money."

"I don't think it's all about the money for them. I believe it's because they don't have something that they feel should be theirs. It wouldn't have mattered if it had only been worth ten cents to anyone else; you had it and they didn't. Even selling out to the land broker isn't about money. I think, and this is just me, that because their father had fought so hard to keep land developers off his land his entire life, they figured that since he didn't want it, then they would have it like that no matter the cost. They're both very selfish like that." Logan asked her why that was so important to them. "Who knows with people like them? I don't think William or Dolly overindulged them, not terribly. They made them go to school, and get good grades too. But at some point it became a game, sort of, for them to do the opposite of the way it should be, no matter what."

"That makes no sense whatsoever." Aunt Georgie laughed and said she agreed with him. "Well, if they come after us again, they're going to wish they had just walked away. I'm not going to allow them to hurt any of us again."

"Good for you. And we'll be right there with you."

He hoped so. Logan didn't think he could stand to see his Charlie in pain like this again.

CHAPTER 9

Walking wasn't nearly as bad as she had thought it would be. Of course, Charlie thought, I'm leaning on everything I can touch. Laughing a little, she tried to stand up straighter and moaned at the small pain that it caused. It was nothing compared to what it had been two days ago when she'd come here from the hospital.

"You're overdoing it again." Walking slowly to the chair to sit down again, she didn't bother saying anything to Zach. He was a constant at the house now, having moved into one of the bedrooms on the second floor. "Want me to get your stool? You're to put your feet up when you're not up and about."

"I know that. You tell me that. Logan tells me. And anyone that comes into his house tells me that." When she looked at the door when someone knocked, she wanted to cry. "Tell them to go away."

Almost as soon as Mason and Emma came into the room, Mason asked her where her stool was. Christ, she was going to murder them all in their beds if they didn't leave her alone. When Zach laughed, Charlie closed her eyes and counted to ten. When she opened them, it was just her and Emma with the baby.

"You want to hold her?" Charlie did, but she wasn't sure if it was too much weight for her to lift. "I talked to the doctor when I took Emily in for her check up this morning, and he said so long as you don't actually lift her but hold her on a pillow, there won't be any problems."

Putting a large pillow over her belly, Charlie watched as the little girl was laid in her arms. Charlie thought for sure that she could take on the world right then and come out on top. Then the baby took her finger into her tiny little hand, and all was right with this fucked up world.

"I've never actually had a lot of contact with children before here. Bonnie is amazing, and I just love how she talks to her mate. Young Patrick doesn't say a word back to her, but looks at her with this look of awe. Even if someone hadn't told me they were predestined to be mates for the rest of their lives, I'd think it was true anyway." Emma laughed and asked how she was doing. "Better. Better all the time, as a matter of fact. Last night I went out on the deck and sat for a little while and didn't hurt all that much. Moving around hurts, but I think I really am getting stronger."

"I talked to my mom yesterday. I wanted to give you a heads up on something. I know that she talked to Logan, but he told her it was up to you. And that Mom had to convince you that it was the right move." Charlie asked her if she was going to be upset. "No, I don't think so. She's planning your wedding."

"My wedding? I'm getting married?" Emma just laughed. "I

don't think so. I mean, Logan has asked. About a million times a day, but I've never said yes."

"Why not?" Charlie told her it was complicated. "No, it's not. You love him. He loves you. What's the complication?"

"This place? Money, or in this instance, my lack of it? A whole list of all kinds of shit that I can't think of right now. And how do you know that he loves me? He told you?" She said he hadn't had to. "See? That's where I get all messed up about things. He told me that he'd had a mate. And I know that they only have one mate for all time. What if he's wrong about me?"

"Trust me, Charlie, he's not wrong." She still wasn't sure. "Why do you think he's wrong? I mean, you have to have some sort of reason for it, don't you? Tell me and maybe I can help."

"Aside from him having a mate before?" Emma nodded. "He's only known me for a little while. If you take out the fact that I've been hurt and out for most of that time, we've had about five days of contact. Yes, we've had sex, and it was fantastic, but there has to be more than that. And he claims that he loves me. Okay, I understand that as a shifter, he has those pesky DNA things that tell him to fall in love quickly and repopulate the world. I don't want him to love me simply because he has this urge to have a baby. No offense."

"None taken. You love him too, don't you?" Charlie shifted as easily as she could on the chair without hurting herself, and nodded at Emma. "So, it's okay for you to fall madly in love with him, but not the other way around. You know that that doesn't make the least bit sense, right?"

"I love him because he's a nice, kind man that has a heart of gold. I don't have the same issues that he might. I can fall in love

125

because someone makes me feel wonderful. Not because they have to love me." Emma told her that she had all those attributes as he did and more. "I doubt anyone would think that of me."

"I do. And obviously so does my daughter." Charlie looked down at the sleeping little girl. "If she didn't like you, she'd let you know. Trust me. Yesterday this creepy guy leaned into her stroller when we were on a walk and Emily screamed her head off. But as soon as he walked away, she went back to being that sweet little baby that you're holding now. Babies have this sixth sense about people. You? She trusts."

She thought of all the things she'd been thinking of over the last several days. There was a great deal of it, too. For the life of her, she couldn't make any of the stuff going on in her head work out. And she was carrying so much baggage, more than most people did throughout their entire life, and here she was with all of this and more and only in her late twenties. Her mother. Her dad. She was going to have all these pending bills from the hospital from being hurt. The nursing facility where her mother stayed was going to be needing more than she could afford right now. She wasn't working so she had no income that she could depend on, and she wasn't sure how to get to a job when she did get better.

"Did you know that Logan has money?" Charlie asked her why that would be important to her. "Because as of the day you were hurt, he had your name put on his checking account, the house deed, as well as the other buildings that he owns in the downtown area. In addition, the credit cards will soon arrive that have your name on them. There aren't many, but there are a few. He's even added your name to where he rents movies, and anything else he has."

"Why would he do that?" Emma said nothing. "You know, this entire family does that. Just waits you out when you ask a question. Like they expect you to get it sooner or later. I don't have a clue why he'd go and do that."

"Because he loves you." It was a good reason, she supposed, but not the best. "And he's taken care that your mom is now getting the best of care where she is. Also, your father now has purpose, and from what I understand, he's getting out of his cell more. Did you know that he's been allowed to have privileges but he's refused them until now? He told Ed, our family attorney, that he'd felt as if he'd not deserved anything after what he'd done."

"I tried to talk to him about it. But he won't let me come and see him but only once a month. And even then, he's so depressed that he spends the entire time just sobbing, asking me to forgive him." Emma nodded. "I miss him. Every day of my life, I miss them both so much."

"I don't know what I'd do if I didn't have my parents around all the time. I can't imagine what you feel. Or for that matter, how he must feel. They're right there, yet you can't talk to them, see them. I'm to understand that they've done some testing on your mom." Charlie told her that she'd not heard the results as yet. "I have them. I didn't ask for them, but when I went there to take care of the incident with her being hurt, they handed me her file and it was in there. I guess when I showed up with an attorney and told them how we were related, they figured they'd help themselves out by handing over what they had."

"Her brain was damaged well beyond what they had thought

at first. I think I knew that from the start. The doctors, they had more hope back then than I did. But they made a believer of me. It wasn't from what my dad did with the accident, but from what happened in the emergency room when she coded. They said they thought that they had gotten her back before any damage had been done. I think I knew for a while now that she...she's not coming back from this, is she?" Emma shook her head. "I thought so. But to have it confirmed, it doesn't make it any easier, does it? I mean I've been telling myself, even before Logan came into my life, that there might be hope one day. My heart wanted it, but in my head, I knew there wasn't any."

"I'm so sorry, Charlie." She nodded at her but said nothing more. Charlie wasn't even sure that she could speak around the large lump in her throat. Her mom was gone.

Charlie realized that she was exhausted and looked around the room. The baby was gone, as was her mom. And the room had a softer glow to it, as if it was twilight now and not early afternoon. Standing up, careful not to do that too quickly, she made her way to the couch only to detour to the kitchen when she heard noises in there. Upon entering the big room, she paused in the doorway to watch Logan. It hit her then.

She did love him. With all that she was. And she'd not lied to Emma when she said that he was a good man. Perhaps a little forgetful, sometimes slightly frazzled, but he was a nice man, a better person than anyone she'd ever met. When he turned and saw her standing there, he came to help her to the chair and asked her how she was feeling.

"Ask me again." He looked at her oddly. "Surely you've not forgotten the question that you've asked me several hundred times a day for the last week. Ask me again, Logan."

Instead of just asking, which she had hoped he would, he washed his hands first, then went to the large mudroom that was just off the kitchen. When he returned, he bent down on one knee in front of her and held out a pretty blue box.

"When my father asked my mother to marry him, he used this ring. Recently, since I've met you, I've had it cleaned up and polished. When I picked it up the jeweler told me that there was a match to this ring, one that had never been picked up, nor had anyone come to ask him about it. But, he told me it had been paid for." When he took her hand in his, she felt her heart fill up. Not with pain but with more love than she'd ever thought possible. "I showed it to my brothers, all of them, and they agreed that the set shouldn't be separated any longer. That you should have them both."

When he opened the box, she could only stare at the beautiful wedding ring set that was nestled in the blue velvet. They were perhaps the most gorgeous rings she'd ever seen. And when Logan took them both out and held them out for her, she knew then that he truly did love her.

The wide band, which she was sure was platinum, was so bright that it hurt the eyes when the early evening sun danced over it. Or it could have been the diamonds, a good half dozen of them encircling the band in a tight circle. The engagement ring was a study in beauty. The diamond, equally beautiful, was held onto the band by a pair of cougars. They held the setting in their paws, their bodies held upward by their hind legs with their tails wrapped around the band and together at the back. The bodies of the cats looked hand carved, and their fur looked like it had been carved by a very skillful hand. And someone that loved their craft.

"Charlie Stone, will you do me the most profound honor of becoming my wife? Will you love me for the rest of my days? Will you live here with me? Have children with me and help me raise them?" When she nodded, he grinned at her. "I'm not done. And in return for you saying yes, again, I will love you beyond my grave. Honor the love you have given me by never straying from you. I will try my very best not to hurt you. Mentally or physically. I will provide for you and your family as if they are my very own. And I will never, so long as I have breath in my body, ever not love you. You will be my world, now and forever."

"Yes." He kissed her then, pulled her mouth to his and kissed her deeply, yet so wonderfully full of love that she held him to her even after he pulled away. "I love you, Logan. I think I have since the day your home burnt to the ground. I love you."

"Oh shit. I almost forgot." He leapt up, then came back to her and pulled her hand to his. Sliding the ring to her knuckle, he kissed her fingers, then her again. She was dizzy with her need of this man, and then he was gone again. When he returned, he handed her a white envelope. "I got this a couple of days ago. I forgot all about having insurance on the house, and when Ed brought me this, I didn't open it because he said it was for us both. I've made sure that your name is on all my accounts too. Anyway, whatever amount this is, we'll use it for our honeymoon. What do you think?"

"Sounds like a plan. And I guess we're having a large wedding too." His face turned such a pretty shade of red that she found that she couldn't be upset with him. "It's all right. I'll just

130

have to tell her that I don't have anyone to sit on my side, and perhaps we can trim her planning down."

"Yeah, good luck with that. Have you met Katie? She's a whirlwind of a woman."

After he made them dinner, they went to the living room and he helped her to the couch. "I love her to death, but she can move a flipping mountain if she has it in her head that it should be elsewhere."

They talked about nothing much. The grapes that were coming in. The way things were getting ready in the barns and how much things cost. As his voice soothed her, Charlie fell asleep. Exhaustion, not just from being up and about but even being in pain, seemed to take its toll on her. But she was wrapped up in Logan's arms, and she felt the best she had in a very long time.

~~~

Roseanna hated being in jail. There really wasn't any need for her to have been arrested nor sent here like she was some sort of criminal. She'd failed to kill either of them, so she should be freed. Had her daddy just done what she'd told him to do then she'd be able to take her brother to the ranch, sell it, and be on her way. This was just stupid.

Roseanna yelled for the police officer again. "I want to know why you're holding me here. And when are you going to let me go." He said nothing. Roseanna was pretty sure that there was something mentally wrong with him. It was as if he just didn't get it, anything that she said or told him to do. "I need to know why you've put me in here. There is no reason for it. I didn't actually kill anyone. And when you finally get around to letting

131

me out, and it had better be fucking soon, I want my knife back. I need it."

"You tried to kill Mrs. Douglas. And Logan too. I don't think you're getting out of here any time too soon." She asked him why not. "Attempted murder. Taking a weapon in an area that is clearly marked not to bring weapons in. Resisting arrest—"

"That sign didn't say anything about knives. And I won't let you hang that crap on me. It wouldn't have been attempted if I could have gotten to either of them before some ass knocked me to the ground. Also, the resisting thing? You know as well as I do had you just let me go when I told you, then I wouldn't have had to hit that other cop when he tried to cuff me." She waited for him to pull out his keys and open her door. "Well? I have things to do. There is a buyer that is coming out to the ranch in a few days, and I need to have this all settled by then. I need to get out of here and fix this."

"You thinking that you're going to be able to sell Logan's ranch?" Roseanna told him it was hers and her brother's. "No, ma'am. I don't think you got that right. I was there when the will was read. Mr. Martin, your daddy, he was right clear on who he was leaving it to. Logan is gonna make that place out there work out. I heard tell that they have plans to sell their wines with the cheese that his brothers—"

"Never going to happen. Daddy wasn't in his right mind when he wrote that up. Not that he ever was as far as I was concerned. Why he continued to make that wine is beyond me. I told him over and over that I didn't want to have to deal with it when he died, and now look. It's just like I told him it would be. Time consuming. And even if he was right in the head, had

132

I known about his changes, then I would have taken care of that before he keeled over." Roseanna thought the officer's face looked pinched, like he was shocked by something she'd said. "I want you to get someone back here that I can talk to. I'm willing to do whatever needs to be done to get what I want."

"You mean sex. Yeah, I heard all about you in school, Roseanna. Trying to trap whatever had an interest in what you were giving out, and even some that didn't, so you could get what you wanted. Well, that's not going to work here." She asked him if he was queer. "Queer? I'm not really sure what you mean by that, but if you think you're going to be blackmailing someone into doing what you want, it won't work. You're stuck here."

After he left her, laughing at her attempts to get him to come closer by taking the top to her jumpsuit off, she sat on the little uncomfortable bed and fumed. Christ, was nothing going to go right about any of this shit? If her daddy was here right now, she'd show him a thing or two about not doing as she wanted. Not that she'd ever hit him, but she'd only have to show how upset he'd made her and he'd change things to suit her.

But toward the end of his life, he'd been doing less and less of what she wanted and more of what Mommy told him. That was why she'd ended up where she had, in a second rate nursing home, so Roseanna could get on with her life. Mommy had always been a hard sell when it came to getting things just right for her.

What nerve Daddy had in changing his mind after she'd made such timely plans. She and Christian were going to sell the land, then go to their daddy's grave and tell him just what they'd done before leaving town again. She remembered the last conversation she'd had with him before she'd left home after the last visit.

"You and your brother, the two of you have no use for the land here and the empire that your mother and I have built up, have you?" Christian just laughed, and she thought of all the times that her daddy had tried to get them to learn the business. Like they cared what he did for a living so long as she was able to tell people that she came from money. "Don't you care that I've worked my whole life to make it so you'd have something to work? Something that your mother and I have built up with our own hands?"

"No. Why should we?" Her father had looked so hurt, and her mother had looked disappointed. "This was your thing, not ours. We enjoyed the money. The fine things that it brought to us. But as far as taking it over, I'm assuming that's what you mean, then no. We don't want anything to do with that part. But the land, selling it, is more in line as to what we're going to do when you croak."

"Croak? My God, Roseanna, have you no compassion at all? I'm a man nearing the end of my life, and you're acting like it's nothing more than the passing of a cold." Roseanna asked him what he thought she should say. "That you love me and want to make my legacy go on. That you'd be proud to make this work, to give all you have to what we're leaving you."

"Daddy, don't be so melodramatic. You make it sound like we're not going to have anything to do with this place after you go. Christian and I have big plans." He asked her what they were. "Do you have any idea how much this land is sought after? I mean, for years now I've tried to tell you that you should sell it. Sometimes, if you want to know the truth, it was embarrassing to see you out there in the rows of grapes working like some common fool. Selling this place? Christ, it is worth a fortune. And even if we don't need the money now, it would really be nice of you to have it sold before you die so we have one less thing to take care of after you and Mommy are dead. I mean, Christ, Daddy…do you have any idea how much work it's going to be to just get you in the ground? Then we have to have the will read. The buyer has to be lined up. Then we have to wait on checks to be cleared. I want you to do all that now, so all Christian and I have to do is just collect what you leave us and move on with our lives. I don't think you've thought of how your holding on to this place is going to inconvenience Christian and me."

"Get out." She looked at her mommy then when she spoke as she stood up. "Get out of my house this moment, and don't you dare return until you have a lick of sense in your head."

"You can't kick me out, Mommy. We need to get this settled. I don't want to leave here without the concrete knowledge that you've done as I want. It's not that much to ask, I think. And if you leave it to us, we're just going to sell it off anyway. Why don't you just move off the land and sign it over to me so I can take care of it now instead of later? We both know that you can't leave this to Christian. I mean you could, I guess, but I'm the one that's going to be running things for him anyway. So just let me line you up with a realtor and a few names, and this will be one more thing off the list of crap that we have to do when you're both cold." Her mommy had walked to the door and opened it, and told her and Christian again to get out. "You're being very rude. I don't know what all the fuss is about. Just do it."

"Roseanna, I never thought I'd say this to my own flesh and

135

blood, especially a child of my body, but I don't like you. I don't think I have for a very long time. I love you, don't get me wrong. But you're the most selfish, rude, self-centered person I have ever met." Roseanna wasn't sure what she was supposed to say back to her, so didn't say a word. "Nothing? You have nothing at all to say to me about this?"

"Like what? That I find you boring? That you're a doormat and a dishrag of a person? If you want the truth, Mommy, I don't like you either. In fact, I don't even think I love you." Her mommy looked so shocked and hurt, Roseanna wanted to tell her not to open cans that she didn't want to taste. "Just tell Daddy to do what I want so I don't have to deal with it any longer. And so you know, you'd better hope that you die before him. I have no more use for you than I do this land and all that comes with it."

Roseanna leaned back against the wall and wondered why this crap kept happening to her. She was just a woman who got things done, and people were somehow offended by it. Christ, did no one see the larger picture? Well, she was going to have to talk to that Logan person. He'd have to sign things over to her so she could be done with the mess her daddy had left her.

CHAPTER 10

Logan rolled to his side to watch Charlie sleep and found himself alone in the bed. But when he looked around, wondering where she might have gone, he heard the shower running. Getting up, he paused outside the door when he heard her crying. He waited, not sure if he should interrupt her sorrow or not.

He knew that the test results had come back on her mom a few days ago. Logan had asked her what she wanted to do now, but she'd told him she wasn't ready to talk about it. Then last night he'd held her while she sobbed, only saying that she hurt and not much more. Opening the door to the bathroom, he stepped into the large room to find her on the floor crying.

She was beautiful. Not what she was doing, crying as if her heart was broken, but beautiful all the same. Her wet hair flowing down her back, her skin slightly pink from the hot water. He couldn't see her wounds the way she was sitting, but he knew that they were healing nicely and that she could get around much better than she had been before. When she looked up at him, he smiled at her.

"What if I washed your back for you?" He meant only to do just that, but when she stood up, turning her back to him, he felt his cock stretch in his boxers and had to adjust himself. "I picked up a few things for you in town yesterday. There is this little shop that Emma and Landon have invested in that makes these pretty little soaps and candles."

"Doris and Tessa. They own Indigo Dreams." He pulled his boxers off and told her she was right. "Emma told me that I should make a trip there when I could. She told me that I smell too manly to be your mate. I wasn't sure what she meant until I realized I was using your stuff."

"I should have thought of it sooner." He took the large sponge, the net kind, off the shelf above his head and filled it with the raspberry scented soft soap he'd gotten. Just looking at her back, the way it connected so nicely with her ass, made his cock hurt. He was trying to think how he was going to manage this when she turned and looked at him. "You're all I think about, Charlie."

"I don't know how this is supposed to work." He asked her what she meant. "Sex with you. I mean, I'm not exactly very put together. I have this ugly place on me that looks like...well, someone did try to cut me open like a can of tomatoes, but I hate that you have to see me this way."

His cat stirred along his body, telling him he could help her with that. When Charlie turned back to the wall, he put the sponge down and turned her to face him. Taking a step back, he stopped her from covering her wounds so that he could look at all of her.

There was nothing about this woman that he didn't love. Her wounds, as she pointed out, did look as if she'd been opened like a can. But that wasn't all there was to her. She was vibrant, funny, and smart. Her skin looked like it had been kissed by the sun, and her freckles, not too many of them, had started to make an appearance. Her hair, wet or dry, was full, curling slightly at the ends to give it a freshness that made him think of summer flowers at the cusp of their season. Silly? Likely, but that was what he felt. But right now, there was a great deal he could do for her. And to her, as a matter of fact.

"We can heal you." She shook her head. "Yes. Not completely, but enough that you won't hurt as much, nor will you scar."

"You mean convert me." He said no, just taste her. "Why didn't you convert me when I was hurt? I mean, not that you had to, but I was wondering about that."

"We didn't know if your cat would have survived it. Both of you might have died had it proved to be too much. Not to mention, we had no idea if we changed you, how your wounds would affect your cat." He dropped to his knees in front of her. "My cat wants to lick you here. Make you heal faster so that he can stop worrying so much."

"You mean, you do." Logan looked at her. "You don't mean you're going to change into a cat and he wants to lick my wounds."

"Yes. I mean that. He wants to taste you too. As much as I do. Taste your cream that you give us when you come." He watched her shift on her feet. "Would you like for him to drink from you, Charlie? Would you come down his throat while he fucks you with his tongue?"

"Logan." He let his cat take him. He wasn't thrilled about being in the water like this, but when she reached over and turned off the water, Logan told him to go carefully, not to frighten her. "He's beautiful, isn't he?"

Charlie curled her fingers in his fur and Logan felt him purr. His cat was moving closer to her, his big body leaning lightly into hers, when he licked her thigh. At her moan, the big cat moved closer to her, turning his head so that he could bury his nose into her apex. Christ, Logan wanted to beg to have his body back so that he could taste her as well.

She came twice before his cat moved between her thighs and nudged her legs wider for him. When she cried out a third time, screaming out her release, she sat on the stall's seat and opened her legs wide. His cat moved to her, lapping at her with quick hard strokes.

Come for him, love. Let him have all that you can give him. She exploded for a fourth time, her body bowing up off the seat as she held tightly to his fur. Even as she begged him to stop, telling him that she had no more, the cat ate at her, taking all that she could give him before he moved back from her and licked lightly over her belly. Then he let Logan take his body back.

Lifting her in his arms, pulling her up to his waist, Logan pressed her against the wall to the shower and entered her. He wanted to go gently, to take her so as not to hurt her. But the moment her legs wrapped around his hips, he started moving in and out of her like a man possessed. He felt that way too, like his body no longer belonged to himself.

Her fingers were everywhere. She touched something deep inside of him with each stroke of her fingers, each time her breath moved over his flesh. When she cried out that she was coming, he pulled her tighter to him, cupping her ass so that he could pound her until she came for him over and over.

"Logan, now. Please give me what I need."

He pulled her hair, adjusting her head so that he could see the pulse as it pounded at her throat. His mouth shifted, his teeth felt longer, sharper than ever before as a human as he sank them into her throat. When she screamed, a sound that echoed around the hard room several times, he tore at her as her blood filled his mouth.

"Again."

His command was met with another tightening of her pussy around him. She screamed again, releasing her climax so that he had no doubt that she was enjoying this. And when she dug her nails deep into his back, drawing blood that trickled down his spine, he came with her. Logan felt his release all over his entire body.

He held her to him; her body was limp, warm but chilling. Stepping out of the stall, trying his best not to fall on his ass and hurt her, all he could think about was that she was his, now and forever. Sitting her gently on the countertop, Logan reached for one of the warming towels and wrapped it around her while trying to keep her from falling over.

By the time he had her hair dried as best he could, Logan wanted her again. But he knew that she was going to be sore; her wounds, while healing, were still there, and he didn't want her to be in pain. As he laid her on the bed, pulling the covers up and over her, Logan stretched. He was sure that he'd not felt this good in years.

"Can you come and lay down with me?" Her voice startled him a little. Looking down at her, seeing the mark he'd given her, he wasn't sure that it was a good idea for him to join her in the bed. "I need you to hold me. I know that you're done with me and all, but I'd like to be held. If you don't mind."

"What do you mean, done with you?" He had a feeling he knew but wanted to make sure. "And I'd love to be curled around you right now, but I'm afraid that I won't stop there."

"But you came." Her face turned a beautiful shade of red and he just barely caught himself from laughing. "What I mean is, you're done with sex for today."

"I doubt very much I'll ever be done with sex with you. I could crawl in that bed with you now and take you to such heights that you're going to think what we did in the shower was only a teaser." She stared at his cock and he fisted himself. "Have you any idea how much I'd like to bend you over this bed and take you hard from behind?"

"Really?" He could see the eagerness in her eyes, smell her arousal like perfume in the room. "I thought.... Well, other men, they just do it and leave."

"Their loss is my gain." She nodded and sat up on the edge of the bed. "Tell me what you want, Charlie. Anything, and it's yours."

When she licked her lips, he wanted to beg her to take him into her mouth. Her breasts were heaving, her nipples were hard as stone and as thick as his thumb. Holding his cock in his fist, sliding up and down it using her cream and his cum, he watched her, waiting for her to make the first move.

"I'd very much like to taste you too." He nearly jerked his

cock off when she licked the tip. "Then I'd like to feel your mouth on my pussy again. I love the way your cat ate me, but you, when you do it, you nip at me and make me come over and over."

He moved closer to her and moaned when she opened her mouth. Sliding his cock into her moist heat, Logan closed his eyes and let her take the lead. As it was now, he was sure he could fuck her throat and come twice before he enjoyed eating her again.

She was a novice. No less sexy or good at what she was doing to him, but he could tell that she'd never had a man in her mouth before. As she touched his balls, almost too hard at first, she got better at it, gentler and braver at the same time. And when she cupped him in her hands, rolling his balls around in her palm, he put his hand on the back of her head and fucked her slowly.

~~~

Charlie loved the textures of his body. Hard in some places, soft in others. His skin was smooth along his cock, while he had furry, thick hair like his cat around it. His chest was softly covered, moving down his body to form a perfect V at his groin. Touching her fingers to each of the places she could touch, she could feel his arousal, not just in the way he fucked her but also his smell. It was like he was bathing them both in his essences.

Fisting his cock in her hand, she marveled that something so thick and long had fit inside of her. Not just fit, but seemed to become a part of her. When he pulled her back, Charlie looked at him, from his hard needy eyes to his cock that still pulsated in her hand.

"I want to fuck you." Nodding, she laid back and spread her legs for him. "Christ, you're so gorgeous. I can't think beyond filling you right now."

"Fuck me." He nodded but dropped to his knees between her legs. When she started to sit up, her body so needy that if he only touched her with his tongue right now she would explode, he told her to be still. That his cat wanted to mark her.

The shift and the bite was sudden. Logan disappeared in a heartbeat and the cat sank his teeth into her thigh. And when he tore at her flesh, causing such incredible pain, she had curled her fingers into his fur to pull him away when she was holding Logan again. Staring at his face, looking into his eyes, she could see something there that she'd never seen before. Love.

"You love me." He nodded, his face never changing while he watched her. "No one has ever treated me like you have. My parents love me, but I never felt what I can see on your face right now."

"You're my world." Nodding, she told him she believed him. "I will love you with all that I am for the rest of my days, Charlie. Nothing will ever come between us, man nor beast. You will be the first thing I think of when I wake and the last thing that is in my mind when I close my eyes at night. My life will be centered on making you happy, keeping you safe, and loving you."

"I love you, Logan." He pulled her to him and kissed her with such love, passion, and understanding that she felt tears fill her eyes. And when he pulled back, resting his forehead on hers, she held him to her and told him again that she loved him.

"I love you as well. And will forever."

Nodding, she pulled away and laid back on the bed. He looked at her then, just stared at her body like he was trying to memorize each part of her. When he stood up, his body no less hard but calmer, it seemed, she moved to the center of the bed and waited for him to join her. As soon as he did, his arms wrapped around not just her body, but her heart as well.

He made love to her then, touching her skin everywhere. Charlie felt as if she were being marked again. His fingers were branding her it seemed, and she couldn't get enough of it. When he moved her face so that she could look at him, she looked into his eyes as he was hers and felt his cock fill her. As they stared deeply into each other's souls, she knew for as long as she lived, this man would never harm her. And that he'd forever love her.

When she came this time, it was with him. Logan held her in his arms, telling her not only with his words that he loved her, but with every touch, every brush of his lips over her skin. And when she felt herself slipping into sleep, he was holding her still, never letting her go even when he fell asleep as well.

Charlie woke sometime later. She wasn't really sure of the time, but it was dark out; not even the moon shining in their room could brighten it up very much. There was the sound of thunder in the distance and bright flashes of light would sear into the room. But it would leave almost as soon as it came, leaving the room in peace and quiet.

Getting up proved to be harder than she thought it would be, because Logan kept pulling her back to him when she got no more than a few inches from him. Finally, with a little pain, she nearly leapt from the bed and moved away. She looked down at the man she'd fallen in love with.

He was handsome. His body was fit, muscled, and tanned. She loved to watch him ride the lines, as he called it. Getting up on his big horse and hearing the saddle creak and moan from his weight was sexy, she thought. But she thought it was the hat

145

that made her wet; when he put it on first thing in the morning, it was all she could do not to beg him to take her right then and there. The man was just too much man for a poor woman like her. Leaving the room before she woke him, Charlie paused in the kitchen.

There wasn't anything in here that she'd not eat. However, the thought of food wasn't high on her list, so bypassing the fridge and cabinets, she grabbed an apple and made her way quietly out onto the deck. The rain was coming soon; she could almost taste it. The big wolf sitting near the steps startled her but really didn't frighten her.

"You must be Paddy." The big wolf nodded and got up to follow her to the swing. "I'm assuming that you're here because of the Martin children. Didn't anyone tell you that they're in jail?"

Again he nodded and she leaned back on the swing. The rain wasn't coming down hard, but she loved watching it dance on the dirt drive. It was a cleansing rain, she thought. Washing away the dirt of the day before to start anew.

"I have to go into town tomorrow. Well, I guess today. I forgot to look at the time when I came out, but I'm betting it's after midnight. Anyway, I'm going into town to sign the paperwork to have the life-support taken from my mom." She heard the door open and looked at Logan when he sat down in the chair next to her. "I was just telling Paddy here that I have a big day ahead of me."

"He told me you were out here. I was just wondering and he contacted me. He said that if you'd like, he can make a connection with you so that you and he could talk if you wish." Charlie said she might think on it. "I would like to go with you today, if you

146

don't mind."

"I wish my dad could be there with her. I know that he blames himself for her being like this, but he wasn't entirely to blame. She had a stroke, one that was coming, the doctors told me, and it was the other trauma that made it happen when it did." Logan nodded; she figured that he'd know that as well. Touching her fingers to the fur of the wolf, she thought about her life after that night and told them both. "When I got the job I'd been dreaming of for what seemed like forever, Mom and Dad came into town to celebrate. They'd never been anything but supportive when I went off to college. Even Dad took on a second job so that he could help me pay for books and supplies while I was there. Anyway, they made the trip in and we had dinner together."

"Your dad, he said that he knew that he shouldn't have been driving that night. The hotel would have been a better route, but he didn't want to spend the extra money on it." Charlie nodded. "He feels responsible for all of it, you know that."

"Yes. He told me that when I visited him in prison. Mom needed all my help by then; the hospital wasn't thrilled about having her there after what they had done." He asked her what had happened. "She was on medications, and they ignored both the bracelet that she had on as well as my dad telling them that she was at high risk for heart trouble. There were plenty of witnesses around; one of them even told me that they'd had a camera right on them when we spoke to them. But they still did things that weren't helpful, and they basically killed her."

"I'm sorry. Did you get help?" Charlie didn't answer him. She had tried everything, but she was just a little fish in a big sea of corporate lawyers. "I'm going to have someone look into this for you. I know that it's too late for your mom, but there has to be a way to get you something in compensation for what they did."

"I'm buried under a mountain of debt. Not only with the hospital, but with every little thing they did to her there that called someone else in. Specialists, heart doctors, you name it, Mom was seen by them over and over until they finally kicked us to the curb and I had to find her a place to be." Wiping at the tears that did no one any good, she thought of what she had to do today. "I have to make arrangements with a funeral home, I guess. Also find somewhere to bury her. I don't have a pot to piss in and I have to take care of this somehow. She should be here with me, not hooked up to every monitor that they can find. I had asked them so many times to give me a prognosis, and all I got for my troubles was a higher bill and no answers."

She felt the swing shift when he sat beside her, and leaned into his warmth. It was a warm night, very nice, yet she felt chilled all the way to her bones. Charlie wondered if she'd be able to do what had to be done about her mom.

"You'll do just fine. I'll be there with you, as well as the rest of our family." She told him that they didn't have to do that. "No, they don't have to, but they want to. And don't be surprised if Ed has a few questions for you about this too. He may seem like a mild-mannered man, but I'd hate to be on the wrong side of him when he thinks an injustice has happened."

"I just want to get this finished. Do something for her when I've not been able to do much else." Logan assured her that she'd done more than most would have. "She's my mom and I love her with all my heart. I only wish it could have been more."

After swinging back and forth for a bit longer, they made

their way into the house. Breakfast needed to be made even though she didn't feel like eating, and then she had to get going. It was going to be difficult, to say the least, but she knew that it was time.

CHAPTER 11

Mason wasn't sure what he was supposed to do. He wanted to hold Charlie, cradle her in his arms like he did his wife and child. But he knew that to do that would have her breaking down, and any fool could see that she was barely hanging on right now. He looked over at Logan when he moved closer to him.

"She's not going to make it." Mason wanted to agree, but he wasn't sure that was what Logan wanted to hear right now. "I don't know that I could do this. Be there when my parent took their last breath, even one that is manufactured by a machine."

Mrs. Stone had been transported from the nursing home to the hospital just last night. He'd had to make a few calls, one of them to Ed, to make sure that they didn't rush through this, turn off the machines before they arrived. He knew that it was to spare the family when something like this occurred, but he felt that it would have done more harm than good with this family. Now Rose Stone was in a private room where they were left to say their good-byes.

Charlie was holding her mom's hand, talking to her in low tones that Mason could hear, but tried his best not to let affect him. There was love there, strong enough to be felt by anyone close. He wondered to Logan how much longer they were waiting.

"The doctor is coming in, and once he's here he'll turn off the machines. And then we wait." Mason asked what they'd be waiting for. "I'm not sure. I guess to see if she just goes quietly in her rest or wakes up. I really have no idea."

The door opened behind them and he watched his wife. Emma had been on the phone since last night, calling in every favor she could. When she smiled at him and winked, Mason turned to Logan.

"Charlie's dad is here." Logan shook his head. "He is. I don't know how she did it, but Emma got him here for this. I think they both need this, don't you?"

When he walked in, Mason wasn't sure what he had expected, but the man standing there with chains on his feet and legs wasn't it. He was tall, almost as tall as him. Thin...a gaunt kind of thinness that went with being indoors all the time, or ill. His hair had been combed out, and it was as white as the shirt he had on.

Mr. Stone was dressed in a suit and tie. It was ill fitting, like he'd lost weight he couldn't afford to lose, and had pulled the suit from his closet only moments before. Before he could tell Charlie that he was here, she spotted her father. The look of shock and happiness on her face was a perfect foil for the things that were going on right now.

The officer with the man was standing back to let them hug

and hold each other. Mason knew that under other circumstances it shouldn't be allowed. That touching at all was prohibited. When Charlie held her father a second then a third time, she turned to all of them in the room with her.

"This is my father, Jason Stone. This is Logan's family." After going around the room, telling him who each of them were, Jason shook their hands. "Landon and his wife, Katie, they're on their way in now. I think that she's planning mine and Logan's wedding."

"My baby girl." Jason held her again, fat tears rolling down his face as he looked at Charlie. "Things would have been so different had I just listened to you."

"It's over, Dad, and you're here now." He nodded, but Mason could almost feel the man's sorrow at what he'd done to his wife and daughter. "The doctor is coming in soon and when he does, you and I will say our good-byes, okay?"

"Yes. I'd like to tell her again how sorry I am." Charlie nodded and Mason looked around at his family again. They were here for them both, he realized, and not just Charlie. When Palmer shook Jason's hand again, the two of them embraced. It was then that he realized that they knew each other.

"He worked for me. When this all happened, I was out of town." Mason asked Palmer if he'd known what had happened. "Not until recently. I knew that he'd been arrested for driving under the influence and for reckless endangerment, but not this. I should have done a better job of keeping tabs on him. There isn't any reason for this man to still be in prison. Ed is looking into this, as well as my team."

Mason could almost feel sorry for whoever got this call. "You

153

think he should have been released a while ago?"

"I don't think he should have been charged with anything, that's one thing. Not to mention, there will be someone there that will be held responsible for this. But not this man. Yes, he made a mistake, but he's paid for that and more. I'll take care of this." Again, Mason felt sorry for that person, but if it got this man out of prison after all this time, then he was rooting for Palmer and his attorneys.

When the doctor finally arrived, the room was quieted. Charlie and her dad stood on one side of the bed while the doctor was near the machines. Mason and his family were surrounding them, knowing that this was going to be one of the most difficult things to happen to any of them, especially Charlie and Jason.

"You know that once this is turned off, there is no going back unless she shows signs of improvement right away." Both of them nodded. "Charlie, I'm very sorry honey, but you do know what the report said, don't you?"

"Yes. She has no brain activity at all. I've already signed the paperwork for her to have her organs and tissue donated should they need it." The doctor thanked her. "Just give me one moment, please?"

"Yes, of course." The man was a doctor that was going to be high on his list of good men. When he stepped back, Charlie took her mom's hand and kissed the back of it. The doctor, not saying a word, wiped at his own tears as he watched her.

"Mom, Dad and I wanted to tell you that we love you with all of our hearts. There won't be a moment that goes by that we don't think of you." Charlie kissed her mom's hand again. "I wish you could meet the people here. The Douglas men are the best you

154

could ever find in friendship. Georgie, their aunt, raised them like you did me. To have respect of others and to be good people. You'd only have to talk to their wives to know that they're very loved and loving people." Charlie turned to her father and he spoke then.

"Rosie, you have no idea how sorry I am that I got you hurt. You will be the only woman that I ever love, and for as long as I live in this lonely world I will regret every decision I made that night." He kissed his wife on the forehead then the mouth before standing again. "You are my heart, love, now and forever more. I love you, dearest."

With a nod from Jason, the doctor turned to the machine. When the beeping started, he touched another button and the silence was there again. As they watched the bright line make its way across the machine, Mason could only think that he wished his own mother was here, so that she could not just hold him but tell him that everything was for a reason. Right now he couldn't see it, but he knew there was one.

After a few minutes, she was pronounced deceased. Then after a bit more, they were ushered out of the room and into another one. Mason asked the nurse that was taking them down the hall what was going to happen now.

"We'll take all the monitors off her body, then clean her up a bit with a brush and one of her pretty gowns. The family will have a little time with her before we take her to the funeral home. Thank you for telling us where to send her." He nodded and asked her to make sure that the bills all came to him and Emma. "I have it on her notes. Mr. Douglas, you should know that there are a lot of us that have been hoping for a better turn out on this.

Two of the nurses that were there that night, they have notes too."

"I think that our attorney would like to speak to them if they're willing." The nurse said that she thought they would, gladly. "Good. I know that some of the things that went on that night were out of their hands, but I think that she might have had a different outcome if they had paid better attention."

"You're right. She would have only had a few broken bones and some stitches. From what I've heard, Jason told the techs that had arrived at the scene, as well as the cops there, that she was on blood thinners and a heart medication." Mason assured her that they'd be very discreet about things. "I honestly don't think they care about that right now. That poor woman should never have been in that home and this happening to her. I'll do what I can on this end, but you can bet that everyone will be thrilled someone is looking into this for her."

By the time they were ready to leave, Mason felt drained. Not only did he have things lined up for Ed, but he had made sure once again that the funeral home had been taken care of. When Logan asked him if he could talk to him about something, he wasn't sure he had anything left in him. Mason just nodded. Family, his family, would do no less for him.

"I wanted to talk to you about the funeral. Ed said you have it taken care of. I want to do this for her." Mason nodded and told him he'd make sure that the bills were forwarded to him. "Also, this thing with her dad. Is there anything we can do right now?"

"I'm working on it." He told him what he'd been able to find out about the staff that had been there that night.

"So you're thinking that we have a good case against the hospital? You have no idea how stressed she is about the money that she owes them. I mean, we were broke, but with ours, all we might have lost was our land and home. She had her mom to think of."

"We'll get this right, Logan. You can count on that." Logan nodded but he looked unsure. "What else is bothering you? It's written all over your face."

"The Martin children. Roseanna is going to be released in a few days. Someone put up her bail money, and her brother is going to go to jail. The trial for him is going to be soon too, I guess. I'm just worried about what she's going to do now that she can be free to roam around. You know as well as I that she's not going to heed the warning to stay away from the farm." Mason had figured that out as well, and told him what he'd heard just that morning. "So she's still trying to sell land that doesn't belong to her. Christ, she's as bad as Dirk was in some ways."

"Yes. But this time I think we're better prepared for something to happen. And legally, she has nothing to stand on. Her father made his wishes very clear. I'm thinking that in the end, this will all be blown over and we can move on." Logan said he wasn't so sure. "Yeah, me either to be honest with you, but we have to think positive. At least that's what I've been told."

"I hope so." Even as his brother walked away, his shoulders just a little lower than before, the weight of all this keeping him down, Mason knew that he was right. Things just seemed to come up on the short end of the stick for them. Not that they didn't generally land on their feet, but it was a hard fence to run when it was going down.

~~~

Roseanna wasn't going to let them treat her this way for much

157

longer. Yes, she was getting out in a few days, but they could still give her a phone and someone to come in and make her little area look better too. The things that she'd had to endure while here were starting to get on her last nerve. The cop coming down the hall had her standing up. He had better have good news for her, or else she was going to have her attorney sue him.

"Miss Martin. I'm afraid that all your demands are going to be left not taken care of. Not that I really think you should have special treatment anyway, but I did ask." She only stared at him, trying her best not to spit at him again. "As for your attorney, he said to tell you that he'd see you the day after tomorrow, and that you're to be good until then."

"I've not done a thing wrong since I've been put in here. And don't think I won't be coming back on this place with my lawyer. You just wait and see." He just smiled at her. "And the buyer, has he gotten to town yet?"

"Oh yes."

That was all he said as he crossed his arms over his fat belly. She was going to wait him out this time, not beg for any information that was hers in the first place. But when he turned and walked away, it was all she could do not to stomp her foot and demand that he unlock her door so she could slap the piss right out of him.

"When did he get here, and when is he coming to see me?" She hated that she had to ask for every little bit of information that she needed. "And I'd also like to know when I can have my own clothing so I can meet with him."

"He's been here for a couple of days. And you're not going to be meeting with him. And you're not getting your street clothing until the judge says you can. You'll just have to wear those until such time as you're released." Her head hurt she was so pissed, and she really was going to hurt this man if she didn't get her way soon. "Also, you should know that Logan is meeting with the man too. Not that you really need that information, but I thought I'd share it."

"What is he doing meeting with my buyer? If he thinks he can make a deal without me there, then he has another thing coming. I've set this up, not him. And I want to take care of this." She put her hands on her pounding head. "I swear to Christ, I could gladly dig my father up and kill him again for putting me through this. I told him, a great many times, to sell out, that I didn't want to have to deal with it. And did he do it? No. He just left it for me to take care of."

"Why is it you think you have to deal with anything? You don't even own the land. I do." Roseanna looked at the man standing there. The cop had left her and this man looked vaguely familiar to her. "Logan Douglas. You tried to kill me the other day with a knife."

"Which no one has given me back. What do you mean meeting with my buyer? I have this all worked out, and you'll just butt out now." Logan pulled a chair from the rack against the wall and sat down. "What do you want? To try and work something out with me? I don't have time for your crap today. I have meetings to attend."

"Yes, I can see how you're all dressed up to go to them too." She wanted to scream at him that it was none of his business, but he spoke before she could. "Why is it that you feel that you have to take care of land that doesn't belong to you and never has? I

159

mean, to hear you talk, your father simply made no arrangements for me to have it and take things out of your hands."

"He didn't make the arrangements that I told him to. It's the same as leaving it for me to deal with. I told him to sell it off, that I wanted nothing to do with it, but he didn't, and now I'm stuck with trying to do what he should have before he died." Logan told her that it wasn't her concern. "How do you figure that? I don't want to be here any more than you do. So as soon as I get out of here, I'm going to get rid of the land and all that crap that my daddy had and go on with my life."

"You're making no sense whatsoever. You don't own the land, therefore you can't sell it off. And once the lawyer sees the will that I have for him, he's going to think you're nuts or pulling a scam and leave you here. Why don't you just back off now and leave the area before someone gets hurt?" Roseanna asked him if he was threatening her. "No. I'm just trying to understand why you're going to all this trouble for nothing."

"I already told you. My daddy was supposed to sell off the land so that when he died, it would be settled. Nothing is the way it should have been. How hard was it for him to call the man I had lined up to talk to and make a deal? Not hard at all. I'd already done all the footwork." She looked him over, the way he was dressed and that ridiculous hat he had on his knee. "What are you, some sort of cow poke? The only thing missing is one of those string ties and you'd be perfect."

"Thank you." She hadn't meant it as a compliment and she was pretty sure he knew it. "I have an appointment with Mr. Carson tonight. He and his attorneys are meeting with myself and the attorneys in my corner. I don't expect there to be much in the way of fanfare, do you? I mean, even though it's against the law for you to sell something that doesn't belong to you, meaning that its mine, not yours, I don't think you're going to go to jail for that. As soon as he figures this out, I'm pretty sure I can go on with my life at the winery with my future wife."

"I have no idea why you think this is going to go in your favor, Mr. Douglas. My father should have done what he was told. Had he done that, then it wouldn't be necessary for me to step in and make it right. And as for you living at the winery with anyone, you know as well as I that you won't be able to do that. The developers are going to level everything and put in some condos or something. It's what should have happened before my daddy left this mess for me."

Logan just shook his head as he stood up. She wanted to tell him to get her out of there, or at the very least have the meeting here where she could have her input, but she had a feeling that he was used to getting things done his way and that was it. Well, she liked getting things her way as well, and the sooner he realized that she was right, the sooner she could get her brother and leave this stupid town for good.

"I almost forgot to tell you. Christian is going before the judge in the morning. I asked a few favors and had it done before you were released. I think that it'll go much easier without you there gumming up the works, don't you?" She asked him why he was going to see a judge. "For attempted murder. He, like you, tried to kill my future wife. But unlike you, he actually hurt her or you'd both be going to prison."

"Prison? For what? He didn't kill her, did he? And she hurt him pretty badly herself. If you think he's going to go to prison

161

for this, then you're dead wrong. Christian is my brother, not some hood that puts him in harm's way. You just tell that judge that I said he's to be set free. He and I have plans, and that does not include me waiting around here for someone to get their head out of their ass and let him go. This is just stupid." He put that hat back on his head. It was tilted just enough that she could see his eyes, and he smiled at her after putting the chair back where he'd gotten it. "You think you can charm me out of this? Well, I have news for you, it's not going to work. I know my rights."

"Do you? I'm not so sure you do. Like for instance, you don't own the property, never did as far as I can figure out. Your father left it to me, all of it, including the grapes and the label that he sold it under. The house, the contents, they're mine as well. I'm not selling, and you can't. It's as simple as that." She stood up closer to the bars that kept her from scratching his eyes out. "You're not going to meet with this buyer, because frankly, you've nothing to sell. Your brother is going to prison, for a very long time if I have anything to say about it, and good riddance to him. You, my dear, are going to either leave town like a good little girl or face the consequences. And trust me when I tell you, there will be plenty of those if you don't do as you're told."

"Why should I?" He asked her what she meant. "My daddy didn't do what he was told, and look what a mess he's left me. And now I have to bail my brother out after I sell the land that Daddy should have sold a long time ago. Do as I'm told? I make the rules, Logan, you don't. And I'm selling my daddy's land, just like I told him I would."

"Well, all I can tell you is, good luck with that."

She watched him walk away, wondering if she told him to

come back to her he would. Probably not. Men like him only knew one thing, and that was what they wanted. They were too stupid to see that she was just as strong as they were and that she had a brain. The sooner he figured that out, the easier things would go for him. And he'd better not mess up her deal. She wanted this taken care of now, not later.

CHAPTER 12

Logan wanted to find Charlie, hold her, then make love to her. Roseanna had made him so angry that he wanted to hit her. It wasn't like him to want to hurt a woman—he knew they were usually smaller and less prone to violence—but right now, he thought that taking on Roseanna Martin might be harder than he'd thought. Logan saw Charlie talking to Percy and Roman and slowed his horse. It wouldn't do for him to go out there, sweep her up in his arms, and take off to the setting sun. When they turned to him, he moved closer to the three of them and dismounted.

"Roman and I were trying to figure out if there was any benefit to having horse manure used as fertilizer. I guess he is going to look into it. They've been using chemicals since he's been here." Logan nodded at the two men who moved away. "Roman said he'd have to sit with you before too long to make arrangements about pickers. I guess they hire some of the locals for it."

165

"Yes. One year not long ago, my family and I came out and helped him. The crop did better than he thought and it was early. I'm not sure what he might have done had we not come when we did. But he sure did throw a nice party afterwards. I think there wasn't an empty belly for miles." She nodded and leaned her body into his horse. "Should you be out here? I don't want you overdoing it."

"I'm fine. I get tired really easily, but I'm not in any pain. I think your cat fixed that part." Her face turned bright red again. "I hope you don't mind about the manure thing. Susie said that they have a surplus of it monthly, and asked if we could take some off their hands. I guess your brother Zach has been using it as well."

"He has. And in a few weeks, he's going to be taking his first crop to my brothers' ranches to sell it to them." Logan watched her. He wasn't as worried about her as he had been, but he was concerned that she'd overdo it. "I did go and see Roseanna. She's a trip."

"She called here, I guess. I didn't talk to her, but she wanted to talk to you or Mason. Apparently she has it in her head that she shouldn't be in jail, nor should her brother." Logan nodded. "When I think about him out there with me.... I don't want to be hurt like that again."

Logan pulled her into his arms and held her. "I don't want you hurt like that again, either. Zach still has bad dreams, he told me. And when you talk to him, you might want to mention how good you feel again." She nodded. "I would very much like for you to go with me to this meeting tonight. I'm meeting with this guy by the name of Carson. He is coming here to buy the vinery, or so he thinks. Ed is going too, just to explain what the will said."

"They're insane, you know that don't you?" He laughed and told her that if he didn't before, he did now. "But for going into town with you, I don't have anything nice to wear. I mean, better jeans than these, but nothing else. I was going to go get a dress for the funeral when I got my check on Friday."

"I have you on all my credit cards, Charlie. Not to mention, there are any number of shops in town that you can go to and get a dress for whatever you want." She nodded and he lifted her chin up to look at her face. "You and I are partners now. In everything."

"Why would you do that?" He asked her what she meant. "You don't know me all that well. And as much as I love you, I think you're nuts to trust an almost perfect stranger."

"You love me?" She smacked him on the arm. "Say it again. I want to hear you shouting it from the rooftops. Charlie Stone loves me, Logan Douglas."

When she didn't say anything, he picked her up in his arms. As he made his way to his horse, all he could think about was taking her. Not just deep in the woods, but taking her body with his. As soon as she was seated on his saddle, he moved up behind her. He knew she was terrified the moment she dug her hands and nails into his hand.

"You're not going to fall." Charlie asked him if he could see how far up they were. "Yes. If we weren't then the horse's hooves would hurt us. This is better than walking." He moved forward a few steps and she screamed.

"You're going to go fast." Logan laughed. He wasn't, but it was fun to tease her. She was the bravest person he knew, and

167

was afraid of falling off a horse when he had her. "Look, this is all well and good for you getting around, but I'm not a horseman."

"No, you and I wouldn't be having this much fun if you were a man in any form." She smacked him again. "I was going to take you out to the woods and make love to you after my cat had his fill of you."

She turned and looked up at him. "We just had sex this morning. Aren't you, I don't know, tired or something?" He shook his head and she turned to look in front of them. "I don't understand you. I mean, you're the kindest man I have ever known, and you like having sex with me. Other men have told me that I wasn't a good lay. Are you just doing this to make me feel better about myself?"

Logan picked her up—no small feat when she was trying her best to hold onto anything she could touch—turned her, and settled her on his lap. With her wrapped around him this way, he knew that not only could she feel his erection, but he could feel her nipples as they hardened against his chest. Lifting her ass up and down, rubbing her pussy over him, he watched her face go from terror filled to needy.

"If you were naked right now, I'd release my cock and pull you down over me while we rode." Her moan had him reaching into her pants and cupping her naked ass. "You're going to drive me nuts; you know that, don't you?"

He tore her pants off. As they fell away, he watched her hands as they worked not just his belt, but the zipper as well. When she slid her hand into his pants and wrapped her hand around his cock, he nudged the horse to move forward, not really caring where they ended up at the moment. Sliding back on this saddle,

LOGAN

he pulled her toward him and held her nakedness to his cock.

"I need you. Can you really have sex with me on a horse?" He had no idea, but he was willing to die trying. By the time he was free of his pants, his zipper nearly unmanning him twice, he could hardly see straight, he wanted her that badly. "Logan, hurry. I need you."

Pulling her down over his cock wasn't as hard as he'd thought. However, she wasn't seated correctly and each time the horse took a step, he'd lose ground. Finally, Charlie wrapped her legs around him and he felt himself sink deeper into her. Christ, he thought that he'd never be able to ride again without thinking of her like this.

Wrapping his reins around the pummel, he held her to him. Each step, each time the horse took a few paces, he nearly came. And when he took a small leap, jumping over a fallen log, Logan cried out. He was having a hard time holding back, just as he'd been the first time he'd had sex with a woman.

Charlie freed her breasts of her shirt. The buttons on his own were scattered all over the ground as she tore it open. When she took his nipple in her mouth and bit down, he held her there, knowing that if she did that again, he'd be finished.

Logan hurt, he wanted to come so badly. His balls felt tight, full, and painfully ready to release. When she lifted her head from his nipple and threw back her head and body, he watched her as she screamed out her release, letting the climax take her away. Logan pulled her back to him and fucked her as hard as he could by lifting her up and down over him until he felt his own climax take him.

Holding her to him while she rolled her hips back and forth,

169

he knew that as soon as they were deep enough in the woods he was going to take her again, but this time he would do it on the ground and not on his big bay. When he started thinking that he was just far enough away, he let her down to the ground and watched her move to a close tree.

"Bring him to me, Logan. Tell your cat that I want him to eat me." His cat stirred along his skin, almost as if he was saying, "Hell yeah, we can do that." "I want him to eat me until I can't stand up, then I want you to fuck me hard."

The cat took him; there was no pause in it as there usually was. He simply went from man to cat in less time than it took his heart to beat. And instead of moving slowly to her, taking his time with his prey, his cat lunged at her, knocking her to the ground and burying his mouth over her wet pussy.

She didn't hold back, screaming out her pleasure each time she came. His cat didn't either, eating her, fucking with his tongue, which had Logan wishing that he could watch her face when she felt it. Logan couldn't taste her as he was, but he knew that his cat was getting as much pleasure from this as she was. And when he moved back, throwing back his head to roar, Logan felt that all the way to his feet. Then he was human again.

Eating her, knowing that his cat had tasted her too, made him hungrier for her. Each time she filled his mouth with her cream, every time she came down his throat, he wanted more, needed more of her. When she pulled his head from her pussy, he stared at her, needing a few moments to understand what she was saying.

"Fuck me." He nodded but didn't move. "Take me like this. I want to feel you fuck me hard and fast. Now, Logan, take me."

He moved up her body, biting her hot dewy skin everywhere he could. And when he was at her entrance, his cock so full now that he was sure that when he took her it was going to be painful, he paused a moment to look at her.

"I love you."

Her nod had him slamming forward, and the climax that he'd been holding onto since he took his body back took him. Even as he fucked her through it, he felt his balls fill, his cock stretch all the more, and he took her three more times, each time emptying not just his body within her but his heart as well. Dropping down onto her, he felt as if he'd been drained twice over and left to die. He didn't even have the energy to move off her. Then he simply blacked out.

~~~

Charlie wanted to get up and stretch. Do a jig and dance naked in the woods. Her body hummed with sexual pleasure, and she wanted the world to know it. Smiling, she held on to the man that had given her so much, and felt her heart melt a little when he snored softly.

She was in love with Logan. She'd known it for a few days now, not just that she loved him, but that he loved her as well. It was hard for her to imagine someone loving her after all the things that had happened. But not only did he love her, he wanted her in his life in all things too. Looking around the wooded area they were in, she watched the deer come out, as well as a few other animals that she'd not seen before, but knew that they belonged to Paddy and his pack.

They won't come any closer to you and Logan. They didn't see the two of you together, but they can smell you. Paddy laughed as he

171

spoke to her through their newly formed link. *You should know that Mason was looking for you both, but I have told him that you are indisposed at the moment. I think he understands.*

I just bet he's laughing at us. He asked her why she'd think that. *I don't know. Logan and his little girlfriend are out in the woods fucking around, when there is a perfectly good bed in the house we could have used.*

Yes, I'm sure that there is. But the animal in him, as in all of our kind, enjoys the freedom of the outdoors as much as we do a good bed. She felt her face heat up. *You are not just his girlfriend, my dear, but his mate. And as far as our kind is concerned, you are husband and wife. The only ones that need the paperwork that goes with him claiming you are humans. And they seem to have little regard for it either. Humans are very strange when it comes to finding their other half, don't you think?*

Yes, but not all humans are like that. My parents, they loved each other so very much. It hurt her to think of her mother dying like she had. Even knowing that she'd been gone for a long time didn't help her. *I have to figure out a place to lay her to rest now. Logan is helping me with that.*

There is a pretty cemetery not far from here. It's been there for generations, and our pack keeps it maintained and safe. She asked him if it was for his pack. *No. It's been used by many people from the area. I believe that even Logan's grandparents are there.*

He never mentioned it. Perhaps he'd rather I didn't use it. Paddy said that he might not know it, or if he did, he'd not thought of it. *It would be nice to be able to go and see her once in a while. I wonder who I would have to talk to.*

You just did. I give you permission, not that you need it, to have your mother laid to rest there. I even know the perfect spot for the two of them when your father's time comes. She didn't want to think of losing her father so soon after her mother died. *I am sorry, my dear. I meant no harm in that.*

No, it's not you. Everything is so fresh yet. Even with her incapacitated like she was, I knew that I could go and see her, talk to her. Now? Well, I guess I can still talk to her, but I can't see her anymore. She thought of her life over the last few months. *I have lost so many people. Mrs. Martin, Mr. Yates. My mom. I miss them all.* Paddy said that he understood.

Logan stirred then, lifting his head from her breast, and smiled at her. She wondered if Paddy had told him to wake up, but when he leaned to her and kissed her, she found she really didn't care. When he rolled to his back, taking her with him, she wondered if they could stay out here forever and hide from the world.

"Emma has some news on your mother's death." She asked him if she knew where they were. "No. And if she did, she'd not say anything. I'm betting her and Mason spend a great deal of time out in the woods too."

She got up when he did. But unlike him, she had nothing at all to wear. So when he handed her his shirt, she pulled it around her and took the cotton to her nose. The smell of him on his clothing made her feel safer, calmer. And when he hugged her to him, Charlie wasn't sure if she should cry or laugh at the picture that they must make.

"You're mine. Forever, love." She told him about the cemetery. "I remember that now. I wondered as a young man why my parents hadn't been buried there. Aunt Georgie told me

173

it was because Mom and Dad had so many friends, both here and abroad, that she was fearful that it would harm the setting of the place. It's very private out there. There wasn't much of them left, just their personal effects really, so I guess that was all right as well."

"I'm sorry, Logan. I forgot that you lost your parents so young." He got up on the horse, which hadn't left them, and put out his hand. "I don't know about this. I'm still pretty far up from the ground when up there."

"I will never let you fall. Not from my horse or at any time. For as long as I live, I will keep you safe, never cause you harm, nor let anyone else harm you. As best as I can." She knew then that he would always be there for her, standing beside her or in front of her. "Come on, love. We should go home."

As they made their way to the house, she told him what Paddy had told her, about the cemetery as well as the wolves that were around the land. He told her that until this thing with Roseanna was cleared up, he'd rather them to be safe than sorry. She agreed.

By the time she had showered and dressed again, dinner was about done. It looked like a lot of food for just the two of them, and he explained that Emma and Ed were joining them. Mason couldn't make it; he was having calf issues, but he might join them for dessert. As soon as they sat down, all of them around the big table, Ed told her what he'd been able to find out.

"The originals of the tapes, and that's what they were back then, were put into a safe. I'm not sure which nurse did it, but apparently just after your mom was situated in her room, she went there and gathered them up. I'm guessing that whoever it

174

was didn't want the medical team to know about it, so she only told one or two people. And it was in her will that they were there." Charlie asked if he'd seen them. "Yes. And you're correct in assuming that they were liable for her recent death too. No one, it seemed by the tapes, had even bothered to read her file nor take into consideration that the medic alert bracelet she had on would keep her alive. They're going to pay, my dear."

"I'm not sure that I want that. I mean, paying off what I owe would be great, and maybe a little help on the nursing home stuff, but I don't know about making them broke." Ed told her that she'd not have to worry about that. "Okay, you do what you need to do then."

"And for your father's part in this, if we can get the courts to agree that the time he's already served should be adequate for what he did, he'll be set free. Not to mention, he'll have a good case against the hospital as well. I plan to go out there and talk to him tomorrow about all this." Her father could be freed? It was almost too good to believe. "I have several witnesses that have signed off on what the doctor did and said. The hospital should have taken better care to look over the information or this might have come out sooner. As it stands right now, they're both sitting in the hot seat."

"I don't understand. How could they have looked them over if this nurse had them hidden away?" He told her that the copies she'd made were readily available to them should they have wanted. "So they might have known that there was a problem and chose to ignore it."

"Sadly, yes. Like most corporations that I've worked with over the years, they try their best not to have to pay out when

175

they don't have to. Even if it means less than honest ways of going about it." Charlie looked down at her plate, overwhelmed by what was going on. "Honey, someone should have done this for you years ago. Things would have been a lot better for you all."

"My mom.... I tried several times to get them to test her. I think now that they were just as happy to have her there, without any kinds of problems, to get money from me. They kept telling me these stories, how she would move her fingers or her toes. No one had ever caught it on the cameras that are in each room, but I still wanted to believe them." Logan took her hand in his. "All this time, all these years, I could have been with my dad. My mom wouldn't have been suffering at the hands of others and we could have moved on with our lives. Not a good one without her, but it would have been better for my dad and me."

"Yes, you're right. And so you know, we have a team going over the files at the nursing home as well." She looked at Emma when she spoke. "There are two more people there that could have benefited from a closer look at their brain patterns. Especially their loved ones and those that were paying the bills."

"So, it's been a scam for a while now." Emma nodded and said that was what they were finding. "How the hell can people do things like this? I mean, don't they know that at some point someone is going to figure this out and do something?"

"Yes, I'm sure that in the back of their mind, they do know that they might get caught. *Might* being the operative word. There is also the chance, in their mind, that they won't. Look how long they were able to string this along without anyone saying anything." Charlie nodded. "Don't feel bad, honey. You're not the first, and I doubt very much that you'll be the last."

"That doesn't really make me feel any better." Emma said that she understood. "So the plan is to sue them for my money back. And in doing this, they admit to wrongdoing and my father is released. Correct?"

"Yes. I would imagine that once this is brought out, there will be a great many other people coming out of the woodwork too. Making claims that their loved one was also hurt in some way." She asked Ed if he meant the hospital or the nursing home. "I think both. Especially the home. And not just this one, but a great many of them will be looking into things that may or may not be true."

"You do what you have to do to get my dad home to me."

Ed smiled at her. It was a very...strange smile, she thought. But before she could think on it too much, little Emily started to fuss from her car seat. Charlie leaned over to pick her up and smiled at the thought of her dad coming home.

CHAPTER 13

"You're saying that she's not even the owner of this land. Never has been." Logan told him that she'd been left out of the will, and that so far as they could find, she had no legal attachments to the land at all. "Then what the hell am I doing here? I mean, I come out here because she had this prime land for sale. And I have to tell you, that land is prime."

"We're aware of that. And we're also aware that you were brought out here under false pretenses. She has it in her head that it's her duty to sell the land off like she'd told her father to do months before he passed on." Howard Carson didn't look any happier about this than he was. "She's currently sitting in a jail cell awaiting her release on bond. I'm telling you this in the event that you stick around for a few more days and she tries to contact you."

"Thank you." Howard got up to pace. Not an easy feat, Logan thought, with the size of the man. He was huge, and not in a healthy way either. "She called me right up about six months ago with this idea that I should come on out here and see her daddy's land. Roseanna told me that her daddy would be calling me soon…he was nearly dead, and she had told him to sell off the property. To be honest with you, I never gave it much thought until Mr. Martin called me one day. Told me that he was right sorry but the land wasn't going to be sold off, but he was thankful that I'd been interested. Well, that sparked my curiosity a bit, and I looked into the land here."

"I'm sure you did. I would have too, I think. But the land, it was never meant to be sold off, and William and his wife left it to me and my future wife."

Howard nodded as he moved toward the big window in the restaurant.

They'd been given a private room in the hotel restaurant. Logan and Charlie had arrived in town earlier to do some shopping and get some things for the house that they didn't have. Mostly it was little things, such as light bulbs and dish soap. But it was the most fun he'd had shopping for such mundane things in his life. Then they'd hit the mall for clothing for Charlie. Looking at her now, he could see that in addition to being beautiful, she held her head a little higher. Like the new clothing had given her a much needed boost.

"She's nuts." Logan felt the burble of laughter spill from his mouth at Howard's words. "I mean, she called me up about two weeks ago, telling me that her daddy had finally croaked—her words, not mine—and that he'd not done a thing she'd lined up for him. I assumed that there was bad blood there. I'd done a little look-see into her life, and figured that I'd be well on my way to being a smart man should I just walk away. But she called me four or five times a day to come on out here and take it off her hands. I'm here because, well, because I wanted to see if it was a sham on her part, and to see if I could get me a good deal. I don't suppose you'd want to sell the land, would you?"

"No. I'm making it work for me. My brothers and I are going to open a few shops around, selling the cheeses that they make as well as the wine and a few other things." Howard nodded and smiled. "I don't know a great deal about wine making, I'll admit that, but I have a good foreman as well as help should I run into issues."

"Douglas Cheeses. Yeah, I heard about you all. Sure did make a man proud to see someone boot strapping it so nicely." Logan asked him what he meant. "Boot strapping. I don't know where the term came from, but it basically means you pulled yourself up by your own boots. Done a good job of it too, if you ask me. Never seen a family so close to the end come back with such gusto. Makes me proud. I'm a strapper myself."

"We had a lot of help." Howard nodded and sat back down. "I'm very sorry about this, Howard. Had I known who you were I would have called and told you what was going on."

"She's not going to stop; you know that, don't you? I'm to understand that she tried to kill you and the little lady here." Logan took Charlie's hand in his and nodded at the man. "You should let her set up a meeting. Let her sell it off and have her head set that she's done what she needed."

"I don't want to sell." Howard nodded and leaned back in his seat. "Ah. You want her to think she's selling you the land, and then have the police come in and take her away."

"I think, and this is only me, that if you don't get her on this, there won't be any peace for you. Me either, I'm thinking. She's nothing if not persistent." Logan wasn't so sure this was a good idea. Yes, she might back off, but if she figured it out, she'd be worse than before. "Once they get her into custody, you and I both know that they're going to figure out that her cheese slipped off the cracker a long time ago."

After they parted ways, he and Charlie had dinner. The restaurant wasn't grand, nothing like that, but it was special. They were on their first date, Logan thought, and he wanted to make sure that she was having as much fun as he was.

"I think his idea is a solid one." Logan asked her why as they finished off their appetizer of calamari and shrimp. "She is a little off. The few times that I've had contact with her, I thought she was single minded. To the point of being reckless about her pursuit in getting what she needs. And no matter how much you try to reason with her, show her where she's wrong, she just doesn't see it."

"You have no idea what it was like to talk to her that day, to tell her that she had no reason to think she could sell off the land that her father didn't before he died, and have her just ignore it for her own need to get it done." Logan ate the last shrimp as he pondered this. "We'd have to have a lot of police there. I'd really hate for Howard to get hurt in this just to get her off the streets. While I was there, she told me that she wanted her knife back. I don't think that's going to happen, but it won't stop her from getting something else."

"True. And her brother, did you know that he's going to go to a mental facility instead of jail after he's released? Ed told me that he's a great deal like his sister in that, but he's more childlike. I think that Roseanna has taken care of him all his life, and he's never gotten to be an adult making adult decisions." Logan had heard that too from his buddies at the station. "Maybe if we can get this rolling in the right direction, she can get some help as well."

"Do you think that'll be enough? Getting her arrested the first time didn't do her much good." Charlie said that they could call in help for her. "You mean other than what we have here. It's a good idea. I think we can have Holly or Emma see what they can do to help out."

They talked about the grapes as their dinners arrived. His was a thick steak, rare, and she had pasta and seafood. They traded bites as they talked, kisses when they were finished, and simply enjoyed each other as they ate their dinner. Logan was walking her out to their car when he thought of something else.

"I talked to Katie about the wedding. She's going to put things on hold until your father is released." Charlie leaned her head on his shoulder and he held her to him. "Katie seems to think that things will go off without a hitch, and when he's out, we'll combine his release celebration and our wedding. Is that okay with you?"

"Yes. Very much so." She looked up at him then. He wiped at the tear on her cheek and told her how much he loved her. "And I love you. So very much."

Instead of putting her into the car, he leaned into her, rocking his cock into her pussy. When she cupped him in her hand, he watched as she used her free hand to lift her skirt up over her hips and show him what she was wearing beneath it. Or what she wasn't wearing. Christ, she was naked and wet for him.

They were in a public place. Though most of the cars had left the area, there were still enough around that they could easily get caught. Pulling off his hat and setting it on her head, Logan dropped to his knees in front of her, and told her she'd have to be quiet.

She was wet, very much so, and the cream running down her leg was still warm. Tasting her there, licking the path back to her pussy, he slid his fingers into her sheath and fucked her while he suckled at her. She came twice, her muffled screams like music to his ears.

Standing up, he freed his cock and lifted her up. This was going to be quick and nasty. As soon as he entered her, Logan felt her tighten around him twice more as she came hard. As he fucked her, unmindful of who might see them—or perhaps that was the point—he took her mouth just as hard, devouring her much like he had her pussy.

"Come. Now, come for me." She screamed then, her breaths burning his skin as she did so in his neck. And when she bit him, sinking her teeth deeply into his throat, Logan came with her, pounding her as hard as he could through two more equally amazing releases.

"Christ, that was wonderful," she breathed. Catching his breath, Logan laughed when she did. It had been pretty good. "All I can think about was we could have been caught."

"I think that was what made it so much fun." They looked over when they heard voices, and watched a couple get into their car as they argued with each other. He wondered, not for the first time, how humans could survive the way they bickered and bit at one another all the time. "In five years, they'll wonder what they're doing with each other and divorce. There are very few marriages that last anymore. It's like disposable tissues. Instead of using a hankie, as Palmer calls them, they just toss them away and think nothing of the havoc that they have created."

"That's sort of sad. My parents would have been married forty years this year. And they loved each other very much. He would just buy her flowers or a box of chocolates because he'd seen them in the store. And Mom would go out of her way to make him his favorite meal even if she didn't care for it." Logan kissed Charlie again. "Logan, let's go home now. I want to just be held by you for the rest of the night."

"Deal." He helped her into the car, making sure she was buckled tightly, and then went to his side of the car. As he was getting in, he saw the couple driving away and that they were still arguing. Logan wondered if asked, whether they would have any idea what they'd eaten or who might have served them. Getting in, he pulled Charlie to him again and kissed her. Just because he could.

~~~

The grapes were beautiful. Charlie caught herself holding a branch of them in her hands just to feel their weight, smell the tangy sweetness of them, and even take a few to her mouth. Percy was laughing at her when she asked him how he didn't have stained hands as she did.

"Because I'm not eating every other one of them I pick." Okay, she thought, there was that. "Also, you keep that up and we might have to supplement our berries with something else."

"The apples, you mean." He nodded. They would add fruit to

185

the wine to give it other flavors. Her favorite so far was the white grape cherry wine. It had a fancy name, she knew, but she just called it the cherry bomb. "The Douglas men have been looking for a building to renovate into a store. Did you know that?"

"Yes. Mr. Logan, he told me to think of someone that I thought could run it well. My father, he would like to, but his English, it's not so good." No, it wasn't, but she enjoyed talking to him in his native tongue just for practice. "My sister, she speaks very well and has a business degree as well. But Father, he thinks she should be married with babies and not working."

"Does she want to do this, Percy?" He nodded, then looked around as if he might have been caught agreeing with her. "Perhaps she could come and talk to me sometime. I've been put in charge of the opening, and maybe if she can work out with helping me, I can talk to your dad."

"He will not be easy to convince. While I love him with all my heart, Ms. Charlie, he is a man set in his ways." Charlie told him they could only try. "Yes. Oh, I'm to ask you about the jellies and jams."

"What do you mean?" He told her what they'd done in the past. "I had no idea that they made jams here too. You think we could make enough to sell that as well?"

"In the past, it was only a few hundred jars that would be given away to whoever wanted it. There are a great many vines this year. The rain and the weather, it has made it so that the vines are heavy. We could easily make the wines and have plenty left over for whatever else you'd like to make. Mother would often come by and Mr. Martin would give her what she needed to make some for us, so long as he was given enough for him and his wife too." Charlie liked that idea. And it would be a good way to make something to go with the cheeses if someone didn't drink wine. "You ever make jelly or jam?"

"No, but I've never made wine either." He nodded, laughing with her. "Can I talk to your mom about this? I don't want her to make it on a huge scale, but she could maybe get enough going that we could sell it in the store as an exclusive item. What do you think?"

"I think that I will be careful from now on when I have an idea. You will...what is it they call it?" She told him. "Yes, you will run with it. I think I'll enjoy watching you talk with Father. He will not stand a chance."

When she saw the truck coming out to the fields, she told Percy that she needed to go. He said that he was sorry for her loss and that he'd be thinking of her. As she got into the truck to go back to the house to change, she took Logan's hand in hers. Instead of talking about what they were about to do, she told him of the jelly.

"I think that Aunt Georgie might have a couple of jars of it left. You'll have to ask her about it. I think it's a wonderful idea. I did wonder what we were to do with all this fruit if we didn't sell any wine." Charlie asked him if he thought that was going to be an issue. "No, I really don't, but then we're coming out under a different label than what the Martins used."

After changing, she made her way out to the porch. The limo had arrived a few minutes ago, and she was surprised to see both Mason and Jace with it. The women, Mason told her, were riding with the baby in a different car. She and Logan rode to the cemetery in relative silence.

There were flowers everywhere. Her father couldn't come, of course, so Logan had hired someone to live feed the graveside service so that he could be there in spirit. As the pack Chaplin stood up to talk about the things she'd told him about her mom, she looked around the area.

There were trees everywhere. And the pretty fence, old and dark with age, had been well maintained over the years. The small wolf, carved from a single tree Paddy had told her, had been put there to keep those that were within the fence safe from harm. It was the most romantic thing she'd heard in a long while. Charlie realized that she'd missed most of the sermon when she heard her mom's name said.

"Rosie Stone, as I said, was a good woman. Loved by those who knew her and respected by those who only knew her in passing. The day she left this earth was a sad day for all. Rosie, may you rest in peace."

Flowers were dropped on her casket. Not the stems, but just the heads. Percy told her it was so that they could reseed and grow a bounty of flowers over the loved one. When she looked around, there were a great many spaces marked by brilliantly colored flowers of every color and hue.

After the casket, a simple one made of pretty oak, was lowered into the deep hole, she stood there, watching the men as they took care to make sure that her mom had a lovely resting place. Even the stone that had been brought out only that morning was beautiful. Her mom's name, along with her father's, was there, with only the years of their birth and her mom's death. Touching her fingers to the cold stone, she thought of all the things that she was going to miss about her mom.

"I know now that you were gone from this earth long ago. I'm sorry for that. The peace you might have felt; I think I did you a disservice by holding onto you the way that I did." She wiped at her tears. "I wanted to tell you how happy I am. Sad that you're gone, yes, but I have a love in my life now that makes your leaving easier. And someday, when we have children, I'm going to tell them all about you and how you were the greatest mom in the world, bar none."

When a chair was brought to her, she sat down and traced the letters on the stone. They were in a nice script, not at all hard to read when she was told what it would look like. The image of her mom and dad on their wedding day had been added behind a thick piece of glass that didn't diminish the happiness on their faces at all. Touching that, she smiled when she thought of the anniversaries that her parents had shared over the years.

"I was just remembering the time that he made you reservations at that bar. He thought the name of it was French sounding. I have no idea how he thought that *pain au fromage* meant steak house, but you told me that the pizza was really good." She had told him days later that it translated to be cheesy bread, and he'd felt so bad that he'd taken Mom out again to make up for it. "He loved you so very much. As do I."

When she realized that they were all waiting on her, Charlie told her mom that she'd be back soon, that she wanted to tell her of her life now. Standing up, she went to Logan and his family and held onto him as they spoke softly, probably the first time in their lives, she'd bet. Smiling at that thought, Charlie told them she was ready to go.

The restaurant was busy, but since Holly had made a few

189

calls and gotten them a private room, they were seated quickly. She didn't have much of an appetite, but she did order. After her menu was taken, she couldn't have told anyone what she had decided on to save her life. But she figured that if she didn't eat it, someone would notice.

"I'm to understand that you wanted to ask me about the jelly." It took her a moment to realize what Georgie was talking about. "I tell you, Marie Jingles can make a jelly that would make you beg for more until you simply popped from it. And she'd always send over a dozen or so biscuits with it just to make sure that we could eat it the way God intended, she said."

"Percy has been telling me all sorts of things that the Martins and his family used to do. I guess one year the grapes weren't fit to use, and he donated bottled juices to the local schools for the kids' lunches. He said that the grape juice that they made was out of this world." Georgie said that it was. "I don't know what I'm doing out there, but I enjoy it. It's so refreshing to be able to be out there in the early morning and work all day at something that I love."

"The others, they say the same. Susie spends a lot of time in the pastures now, getting the ponies ready for sale. Emma has branched out as well; she's taken on a few projects as mayor that this town has needed for a long time. Even Holly, in her advanced state, gets more done in one day than most can do in a week. That baby is going to come out ready to get to work, I swear it." They both laughed as they watched the woman move about the room as if she wasn't large with child and overdue by nearly a week. "Have you and Logan spoke of children yet?"

"No. I mean sort of, but only about little Emily and how

190

much fun Mason is having being a father. Emma acts like she's been doing it for years. I guess that stems from having her mom so close at hand." A sadness washed over her then, not as painful as it had been earlier, but it still hurt some. "I'd like to have them. Several as a matter of fact. I was an only child, so I don't want to do that to my children. It's somewhat lonely. Or at least it was to me."

"I had my brother when we were younger. He was wonderful to the boys, and to his wife too. Zelma and he, they had a storybook love affair. And when the kids came along, you would have thought that they'd been given a gift that could never be outdone." They both watched the men now bantering back and forth about something that was said to Zach. "When they died, it was difficult for me to come here. Not that the boys ever made me feel anything bad for taking them in; they gave me everything they had because they were raised by good people. I felt bad because I knew that I'd never be what they had with their mom and dad. In my heart, I knew that I'd never be enough."

"I think you were more than they could have hoped for. I know that Logan thinks of you as someone that he can depend on. He loves you with his heart and soul. And you did an amazing job, not just in raising them, but making them good men. Men to be proud of and love." Georgie nodded and Charlie could see that she'd made her cry. "I'm sorry."

"No. No, you did nothing wrong. I was just thinking about how much I'm going to love having you in this family. You're going to be good for all of them. Zach, I think he'd marry you himself for the friendship that you've given him. The boy nearly shines with it." Charlie and Zach had become very good friends.

191

And she told Georgie she was glad that no one was upset about it either. "There is no reason for them to be. You've brought him out of his shell. Why, a few months ago, he would have been standing back and taking the guff that his brothers gave him. Look at him, right in their faces like he'd take them on."

"Oh no. Oh no. Oh no." Everyone paused in whatever they were doing to look at Holly. "I think.... Jace, it's time. We have to go."

The movement from the dining room to the cars in the drive was made quickly. Before she knew it, Charlie was in the back seat with Holly and Jace was driving them, including Logan, to the hospital.

CHAPTER 14

Logan looked down at his first nephew. Christ, he looked so much like Jace that he was sure it was him he was looking at. The only thing the little guy had gotten from his mom, it seemed, was her dark hair. But the bold hard chin, the way he just laid there like he had not one care in the world? It bespoke Jace all the way around.

"You think he looks like his mom?" Logan only stared at Jace when he spoke. "I think he looks like her a lot. I hope he has her smarts too. Isn't he the most perfect little thing you've ever seen?"

"Yes. And no, he looks just like you. I think he's thinking right now that it's too bright in this room. That the other children need to be quiet, and that he's wondering where his next meal is." Jace grinned. "You do know that none of that was a compliment, don't you?"

"I don't care. I have a son." Logan looked again at the little baby with Douglas taped over his head on the bed. "I asked Holly when we could have the next one and she hit me. Can you believe that?"

"I think I might have shot you. Weren't you in the delivery room when she called you every name in the book? I thought for a moment there, when the doctor said it wasn't time for her to push, that she was going to come up off that table and knock the shit out of him." Jace nodded again, the grin on his face nearly as wide as his head. "I think it might be months, if not years, before she ever lets you touch her again."

"She loves me." That much was true. Holly did love her mate. "Thanks for being there for me. And Charlie sure did keep things from getting out of control when Holly said that she wanted to shift and eat the nurses. I think for a moment they believed that Holly would. But Charlie laughed and said she was in a lot of pain."

"I don't think that Holly was kidding, do you?" Jace grinned even larger, shaking his head this time. "Yeah, you need to be a little less happy."

"I don't think I can. Wait until you have a child. I'm telling you right now, it's the greatest feeling on earth. And when you get to hold him? I'm telling you right now, Logan, the love that seems to grip you so hard will take your breath away the moment that he looks up at you." Jace turned to him then. "I was just headed back to the room. Wanna come with me? I got something for Charlie for being there with us. And for you for keeping me from falling over."

"You didn't have to do that. I think we both enjoyed it." Jace said he wanted to. As they made their way down the hall to the rooms, Logan could see the rest of his family spilling out of the room. "You have a name yet? Because if you don't, you'd better think of one really quickly. They're going to draw blood if you don't tell them."

"We got it." Logan asked him what it was. "You're going to have to wait with the rest of the family. But I think you're going to love it as much as we do."

As soon as they entered the room, Logan looked for Charlie. She was huddled in the corner, sort of distancing herself from the rest of them. She'd told him last night that when they were all together like they were now, it was almost too much for her. She wasn't used to being around large groups of people. And they were a large group.

As soon as the baby was brought in, he was handed off to Holly. Everyone seemed to want to crowd the couple, but they were restraining themselves. It wasn't until Aunt Georgie made her way to the bed and asked to hold him that Holly smiled at them. The little man was handed over and promptly laid on the bed and uncovered.

He really was perfect. Ten fingers and toes. The cutest little button nose. A head full of the darkest hair he'd ever seen, and so much of it, Logan was sure that it could have been pulled into a small bun. And when he stretched out, his little hands up over his head, Logan fell in love with him, just like that.

"Everyone, I'd like to introduce you to our son, Palmer Norman Douglas. Named for some of the greatest men that have ever lived. We've decided to call him Pal for short, but I'm sure with a handle like this one, he'll have an endless supply of shorter versions of his name." Their father and Holly's dad. Yes, it was fitting. They were great men and now they had a legacy to live on long after Palmer was gone. "And we're happy to announce that he's cat, nearly full bloodied."

After that, little Pal was passed around so that each of them could get his scent. When Logan saw Charlie holding him, he felt his cat stir. The need to see her fat with his child was overwhelming. But he'd have to talk to her first. He had no idea how she even felt about having children.

~~~

Roseanna sat very still in the restaurant. She wanted to get up and demand that someone find out where this Carson person was, but she was told she had to behave until she was ready to leave town. But if any of them thought she was leaving here without her brother, they were surely mistaken. The officer that had released her earlier had told her that she wasn't going to be able to see him until after the trial.

"What trial?" He explained what her brother was supposed to have done. "That's the stupidest thing I've ever heard. He didn't kill her, and I think that should be more than enough to have him released. Christ, you'd think that he was some sort of bad guy the way you all are treating him."

"He is a bad man. And he's going to prison for at least ten years if not more." It was well within her rights to smack him, she thought. This was the second time within an hour that someone had said that Christian was going to go away for a long while. "If he's found to be competent to stand trial that is. The hearing on that is over, we're just waiting on the results."

"Christian isn't nuts. He might be a little sensitive, but he's far from being crazy. I want you to go and find that doctor that tested

196

him and tell him that I'll answer the questions for my brother. I don't have time for this crap. As soon as I meet with this Carson person, we're leaving town." He told her that Christian wasn't going to be leaving. "You heard me. I want him released so that we can get out of here."

Nothing, not one thing that she'd done, had gotten her what she wanted. And now she was going to sell her daddy's land and have to wait around for someone to get their head out of their ass and let Christian go. As she drummed her fingers on the table, trying her best not to call the man again, she thought about her conversation with Howard.

"I'm here now. I arrived about two days ago. I thought you said this was going to be an easy sale." Roseanna had called him the moment she was released, and when he'd answered the phone, Roseanna had demanded that he get to her. "I really should get back to my ranch, Ms. Martin. This is taking up more time than I thought it would."

"You're going to meet me at the restaurant in an hour. When you sign all the necessary paperwork, then you can leave town. I don't want to be here anymore than you do. And wouldn't have to be if my father had simply done what he'd been told." He didn't say anything, and that had pissed her off. "Look, I'm a busy woman and I want this sale finished. You either show up or not. It's up to you, but I will sell this today."

"I'll be at the restaurant on Tenth Avenue at five-thirty. I have things to do as well."

Then the phone line went dead. It was well within her rights, she thought, to have hung up on him. And she might have called him back to do so if she hadn't needed to find her brother. These people were going to have to get on the ball around here.

And here she sat, no closer to finding her brother than she had been before, and no one would help her find him. Someone was going to have to tell her soon. When she sold her daddy's property, she was going to go back home.

Home. She thought about her home that she shared with Christian. They had been living there since she'd been moved out of her family home about ten years ago. Her daddy had said it was for the best, separating her and Mommy once and for all, but she'd thought things might have gone better for her had her mommy moved out, not her. She certainly wouldn't have had to be here today. The property would have been sold sooner, her mommy would have...well, Roseanna had no idea what she might have done with her mommy had her father not kicked her out. Probably they would have ended up screaming at each other all the time, much like they did before.

Then the money had stopped coming in. Her daddy had said he'd make sure she and Christian were taken care of. She had a job, not much of one but she had it. And Christian had worked when he could. The fact that they'd not had to pay for their housing nor their utilities hadn't occurred to her until someone had shown up at their door to tell her she was behind in payments.

"I don't do that." The man, someone in a ridiculous uniform that was too small for him, had told her that no one was. "Call my daddy's attorney. He's the one that takes care of it."

"He said that you're no longer going to receive money from the estate. As of right now, you're over six months behind on your electric bill. We'll need for you to pay that now or I'm to shut it off." Shoving him off her front porch, she stomped over to his truck and slashed the tires. "What the hell do you think you're doing? That's going to cost you."

"You turn off my power and there will be worse." It was a mistake to let him pull out his phone, she realized that now. And when he told someone on the other end of it what she'd done, she wanted to laugh. Roseanna thought that she'd won that battle.

However, she'd had to spend two days in jail, plus pay for the tires. Well, she'd not paid for them, but the stupid company had had permission to take the money right out of her account. And the money for the electric bill too. And while she was gone, someone had gotten Christian to pay not only the cable bill that was past due, but the rent as well.

When she finally heard from the attorney, after calling for nearly a week, he informed her that her daddy had died. While he went on about how great of a man he was, that he'd been a good client as well as a friend, she wondered how this was going to affect her. When he finally shut up, she spoke.

"Did he do like I told him? Sell the land?" The attorney said that he'd not been aware that it was for sale. "Well of course it is. I told him to sell it so that I'd not have to deal with it when he finally died. Where is Mommy? Is she dead yet?"

"No. Your mother is still living in the house, last I heard." Roseanna said she'd take care of that. "I'm sorry, Roseanna, what is it you're going to take care of? And you should know that your father's will is scheduled to be read on Saturday."

"I can't make it. Just plop him in the ground and set up a time when I can come out there and take care of the house and land. Why he didn't do what I told him is beyond me." The attorney said that his arrangements had been made. "Well, he did do something right, didn't he? I'll be out there in a week. Just make sure that the house is emptied by the time I get there."

Not only had the house not been empty, but her mommy was still living there. Getting her committed to one of those nursing homes hadn't been a problem, but everything else had been. No one was doing as she wanted.

"Ms. Martin? I'm Howard Carson. We're to talk about this land deal you have?" The man loomed over her so she stood up. Taking his hand in hers, she waited for him to sit so she'd not have to look up at him. "I have to tell you, after talking to Logan, I was surprised to hear from you. Did he sell it back to you?"

"There was no reason for him to sell me anything. The land was my daddy's, and I need to unload it. I hope you're not going to try and give less for it than we agreed upon." He said that he'd never agreed to anything. "I want fair market for it. Before I just wanted to unload it, but I think that with my current situation, I want money. You'll pay me cash up front for this."

"Okay. But I want to make a few things clear right off. Logan said that you have no rights to sell his land." She started to tell him that Logan could go fuck himself, she was doing what her father should have done when she told him to. "Let me finish. You do know that if you have no rights to this land, that it's breaking the law? And that by selling it, it's the same as theft."

"My daddy is dead. The land, which I told him to sell, is just sitting there. Are you going to buy it or not? I swear to Christ, if he wasn't already dead, I'd go find him and beat him to death with a chair." Howard only stared at her. "Well?"

"Yes, I'll buy the land if you own it." Shoving the paperwork at him, she waited while he read it over. She was glad now that she'd made a copy of the paperwork she'd left for her daddy before he had croaked so she'd not have to find someone to write this up for her again.

When he pulled out his checkbook, she told him that she wanted cash. That way she'd not have to wait to see if his check cleared, and she could use it to grease a few palms to get information on her brother. He was here somewhere, and when she found him, they were going to go home.

"I don't have that kind of cash on me. You think I can carry around four million dollars in my wallet? That's just stupid." He had a point, and as much as she hated to admit it, she'd never thought of that. "I can give you about a thousand dollars in cash. That's about all I have on me."

"Fine, I'll take it. You just make sure that you don't try to adjust the amount on the sale. You should have thought of that before you got here." There wasn't any way she was going to admit that she hadn't thought of it before. "And when this is done, you can buy me a dinner. I deserve it after all the shit you and the rest of the people in this town have put me through."

Signing her name to the paperwork after he did, she felt like something, one thing, was going in her favor. And when he handed her the cash, ten one hundred dollar bills, she shoved it in her purse before he could change his mind. Not that she'd allow that, but she wasn't taking any chances with something going wrong. But it did, quickly.

"Roseanna Jane Martin, you're under arrest for felony of the first degree, or aggravated theft. You have the right to remain—"

"What the fuck are you talking about? Unhand me, you fool." The man in the dark suit jerked her arms behind her and cuffed her. The sound of it, the zipping sound, was loud in the room. Every person there, from the waitress that had been sloppy at her job all the way to the man sitting across from her, was staring at her. "What the hell are you looking at? Get away from me and let me go before I have to hurt you."

As he droned on about her rights and attorneys, she could only think that she was being detained again. But no matter how many times she told them to let her go, to get the cuffs off her, no one would do it. Then she was being dragged, quite literally, out of the restaurant.

"Get my money and the contract. When you let me go, I'm going to have to cash it and get my brother. And don't think I didn't notice that none of you have mentioned him either. I want him here now." The man just laughed and she rammed her head into his face, bloodying his nose as well as his lip. "I will not be laughed at. I want Christian here now, and I want you to let me go."

"You're not going to be let go this time, I'm afraid. Charges have been pressed against you. Not just on the felony, but also the battery charges that Mr. Wayne filed this morning. Also Mrs. Hamilton at the diner and Mr. Douglas…Mason this time, not Logan." She told him she didn't know who those people were. "Well, Wayne owns the hotel where you were staying. This morning when he asked you for another credit card for the room, as the one you had used was denied, you knocked him down a flight of stairs, then stepped on his head. Mrs. Hamilton said you hit her with a plate, claiming that you shouldn't be charged for such a meal when you never got your cappuccino. She tried to tell you that they didn't sell those before you busted her face."

"I don't care what she said. Had she just given me what I wanted, then I wouldn't have had to hurt her. I don't understand people. If you're going to say you have coffee, you should have the right kind of coffee." He just shook his head. "See, you agree. And this other person. What does he claim I did?"

"You spit on him. Right after you bumped into him on the sidewalk." She asked why spitting was a crime. "It's theoretically considered assault. But with all this other stuff going on with you, I'm pretty sure we can make this one stick to you like…well, like slobber."

These were by far the stupidest people that she'd ever encountered. And no matter how many times she told them to let her go, she was still put in a cruiser and locked in the back seat.

What was wrong with people nowadays? Every little thing would send them to an attorney. All she'd wanted to do was get her daddy's place taken care of, like he should have done in the first place, and leave here with Christian. Now she was being treated like she'd done something wrong.

Within moments of arriving at the jail again, she was placed in a room with only a big mirror. She knew that someone was on the other side of it, and stuck her tongue out at them several times while she waited for someone to come and release her. When the door finally opened and there stood someone she didn't know, Roseanna turned her back on him.

"I want my brother so we can leave here. And my money. Howard bought my daddy's land, which is the only reason I'm here, and as soon as you let me go, I'll be on my way with my brother." She glanced at him when the chair scraped over the hard floor. "Don't get comfortable. I want Christian here so we can go. And my check. Don't forget that. And I know that you took my money too. That will be returned as well."

"There is no check. And the money you received has been returned to the rightful owner." She told him it was part of the sale and it was hers. "I'm afraid not. The sale of the land that you did not own has been cancelled. You didn't own the land, nor were you able to sell it. The deal was null and void."

"So you tricked me. Not nice. When are you going to let me out of here so I can sell the property? My daddy should have done it before he died, like he was told, but he didn't. I have more important things to do than to just sit here when I have shit to do."

"Why is it you think you have to be responsible for your father's land? He took care of it the way he wanted to before he passed away. There was no reason for you to take it upon yourself to do anything with it." She pointed out that he'd not sold it like she'd said. "I understand that. He willed it to Logan Douglas, the rightful owner of the land and the house. Why didn't you just leave well enough alone?"

"Because he was supposed to sell it so I'd not have to deal with it." She turned in the chair and looked at him. "Don't you understand anything? If I didn't come out here and take care of this, the way I wanted him to, then it would just sit there. The land needs to be sold off so I can move on with my life."

"But it wasn't yours to sell." Roseanna wanted to hit him. He simply wasn't listening to a word she said. "You were informed that the land wasn't yours. By several people, as a matter of fact. There was no reason for you to come here, no reason at all for you to line up a deal with Mr. Carson. Had you not, then your brother wouldn't be facing attempted murder charges and you'd not be facing a jail sentence for a felony like you are."

"First of all, Christian didn't kill that woman. She's still up moving around; and where is he? No one will tell me. For all I know, you've made up some trumped up charges and are holding him against his will." He told her where her brother was. "I don't want him to be locked up in a mental institution. You are to bring him to me right now so that we can line up another buyer to get this business finished."

"You aren't leaving here, Roseanna. Nor is your brother. He's going to be institutionalized for a very long time. I would imagine that you will be as well." Roseanna held her head. It was spinning hard and she thought they'd given her something, and asked him about it. "No one gave you anything. You've not drank or eaten anything since you've been here."

"I want my check and money so we can leave. Christian needs to come here so we can leave." She was getting sicker by the moment. Now she had to hold her head tightly in her hands so that it didn't explode. "I have business to attend to, so I demand that you let me go so I can do it."

Her eyes felt too big for her head. They were burning too. They were doing this to her, these men. And when she looked at him, the man again, he blurred out twice before she could get him into focus. Everything was hurting now, and she laid her head down on the table.

"Roseanna? Roseanna? Can you hear me?" She hushed him; it was too loud...his voice seemed to be ringing in her head. "Roseanna, can you hear me?"

"Too much. I need to.... Let me go so I can go home with

Christian. After that, we'll come back later and fix this sale."
Blood was pooling at her nose. Sitting up caused her to feel sick,
but she held it down. "I don't feel so well."

CHAPTER 15

Logan hung up the phone and sat down at the table. Charlie was still outside in the barns, and he had come in ahead of her to fix dinner. The phone call, while expected, wasn't the information that he'd hoped for. As soon as Charlie came into the house, he looked at her and she sat down.

"What happened?" He shook his head, still in disbelief. "Logan, you're scaring me. Is it my dad? One of your brothers? Tell me the babies are all right."

"Roseanna Martin had a brain hemorrhage about an hour ago. They took her by helicopter to the larger hospital about an hour from here and she was taken right to surgery. She passed away ten minutes into the operation. The blood loss, as well as the swelling in her brain, was just too much." Charlie leaned back in her seat, looking much like he felt. Pole axed. "That was Wendell, he's a doctor at the hospital. He said that they found a tumor about as big as a walnut pressing against her brain. And it had been there for some time. He said that they think that it just became too large for the space there, and that's what caused her to bleed out like she did."

"Did she suffer much?" He told her that once she passed out at the jail she never woke up, so he didn't think so. "That poor woman. I didn't like her very much, but I hate that she died like this. Don't you?"

"Yes. I don't know if that explains her one track mind on this entire thing, however. Wendell said that they might never know." Charlie nodded, stood up, and went to the fridge. "I don't feel like making anything. Do you want to just order a pizza or something?"

"Family." He asked her what she meant. "We need family here. Or at their home, I don't care. But I'd very much like to be surrounded by your huge, loud family for a little while." She moved to the door then. "And food. I'm sure that if we call them now, someone somewhere will get something started. Even if it's just sandwiches."

He reached for his family as they made their way to their car. When Mason laughed and told him that Emma had been thinking the same thing, it was settled that they'd meet up at his house. Their butler, he told him, would have things started.

They were all there by the time he stopped and picked up several bags of ice. Even Landon and Katie had come over, as well as Paddy and his family. It was perfect, Logan thought. Just exactly what they all needed. By the time they were ready to eat, he and his brothers had set up several long tables in the yard and all the drinks were iced down. It was time for some chowing down.

There was so much food, Logan wondered if they had been planning this. Not only were there burgers, but steaks, chicken, and ribs. In addition to green beans, peas, carrots, and potato salad, there were enough desserts to have the food table groaning. Mason had asked the staff to join them as well. Logan was just ready to unbutton his pants to be able to breathe when Zach sat down next to him.

"I have an issue I need your help with. But you have to promise me that it's just between the two of us." Logan said that it wasn't a promise he could make, in the event that it was bad. "It's not. Not really. Just…I have been keeping a secret. A big one, I think."

"I promise that I'll keep it a secret so long as you're not in trouble, nor will it harm any of us, including you." Zach told him that was fair enough. "You're not in trouble are you?"

"No, nothing like that. I'm having trouble is more like it. You see, I bought a building recently. Like in the last few months." Logan nodded, thinking this was going to be bad if his very tight fisted brother had bought something so huge as a building. "I purchased the building from the city for a buck. Not even Emma knows who has it. Not yet anyway. I worked with Ed and got it under a corporation name that was simply Childlike. And when it's finished, if that ever happens, I hoped it would be used as a home for children and their families who come out to see the ranch that Susie and Gerard run."

"That's wonderful, Zach. I love that idea. I'm assuming by your face that some kind of snag has tied you up." Zach nodded and glanced at Emma. "She's stopping you?"

"Not her. Emma wouldn't do this to someone. But her staff,

209

particularly her secretary, Beth Rogan. I've tried to go the right way in with this. I've gotten all my permits lined up. An out of town construction crew ready to go. I even took out a loan to get the building inspected. Nothing was out of order, Ed made sure of that." He asked him what it was then. "Her secretary is threatening me. And as much as I'd like to go over there and tell Emma what's going on, I don't want to be made to feel stupid."

"Why on earth would you be made to feel that way?" Zach's face turned pink and he looked down at his feet. "Zach, don't make me have to hurt you to get answers."

"Beth said that the building is condemned and that my permits were gotten illegally. When I asked her how, all she told me was that should I just let it go, so will she. I'm still not sure what she meant by that." That didn't sound right. "Logan, I think she is trying her best to ruin Emma too. I've…Ed and I have been looking into things. There is some serious shit going on in that place."

"You need to tell Emma." He said that he had no proof. "Who cares about proof if you have knowledge like this? Emma has to know, even if you just tell her about the things you've found out with Ed."

"Ed said the same thing. There is some serious embezzlement going on, as well as on a few of the contracts that the city has, the people are being handpicked, and not by Emma." Logan wasn't sure how that worked, but said nothing while Zach continued. "I think, and this is just what Ed and I are tossing around, that the reason that she doesn't want that building going in is because I have my own crew working on it and not someone that she's hired. It's not a city project but my own. I think she's afraid that my crew will show the city what is going on."

"So what does Ed think is happening? And what do you mean, the city will see what's going on?" Instead of answering him, Zach handed him several pictures. They were all marked with dates and another number that he didn't understand.

"The dates are when the project was supposed to be started. The number is the contractor number. All bidders are assigned one when they bid on a city project. That number is the only one they'll get, so the city can keep track of who bids and how much." The dates on some of the pictures were years old. Zach said the pictures were of the projects as of the day before yesterday. All the bidder numbers were the same. The pictures showed that while some of the project start dates were well over three or four years old, nothing had been done about them. "When I was inquiring about this, picking up as much information as I could in the lower levels of the courthouse, I overheard Beth tell someone that Ed had to go, he was too nosy."

"Did they see you?" Zach said he wasn't sure. But Ed had started going places with someone with him at all times. "Good. We'll have to get him more protection, and you as well. Emma needs to know this. Hell, Zach, everyone does."

"I know." He still didn't look convinced. "What if I'm wrong? What if my paperwork is messed up? Perhaps I just misunderstood her."

"Do you really believe that?" Zach looked at him and shook his head. "I don't either. This is the perfect time to tell everyone. We're all here and we can help you with this."

It took nearly two hours to get the whole story out. Emma was shocked to say the least. And when Ed arrived, a thick file in his hands, he passed out copies of what he and Zach had unearthed in their search. The contractor was Beth's father-in-law, Joseph Rogan.

"Most of these projects have been shoved under the rug. Two of them, the school playground as well as the park near there, has been turned over to the city attorneys. This was several years ago, and now is just sitting on someone's desk, I think." Jace asked Ed why they were just finding out about this. "More than likely, the other mayor knew and was taking a kickback for not mentioning it at town meetings. But when Zach had me look into a few things for him, the building that is getting this out in the open, I found a lot of other items that have not been taken care of. New ambulances for one. There was to be a clinic set up for young pregnant women that I can't find paperwork on, as well as a couple of other minor things."

"This isn't new. I mean, wasn't this something that was brought up in a couple of other cities across the state? The contractor related to someone in office, them getting caught, and no one really serving any time." Ed mopped his face with his handkerchief as he nodded at him. "So now what do we do?"

"We have to be careful." Everyone turned to Palmer, who had been quiet until then. "In order to get all parties involved, we have to just lay low and wait them out. We don't want them to run, nor do we want the same thing that happened in our town before. Scandal and death. And there will be if this comes out. We're talking millions of dollars here, a great deal of money to think they're going to go quietly into the night."

After plans were made, most of them between Palmer and Ed, things settled back down to normal. Or as normal as their family could get. When Zach stood up, to no doubt leave, Mason did as well.

"I wanted to thank you, Zach. Not just for this information — you might have saved a few lives with this — but the building and your project. You did something none of the rest of us thought of." Zach glanced at Logan, and he could see the accusatory look on his face. "He didn't tell me to do this, if that's what you're thinking, little brother. I love you for this. And am proud as I can be that you've taken this on. However, I would also like to lend my support in any way you need. Financially or physically. You have it."

The rest of them offered him the same thing. Zach was so embarrassed by the time he left that Logan wanted to laugh. Poor guy, he'd done a good thing and was too shy to let them all know.

~~~

Tisha made her way to her new classroom. She loved the first day of school, and tomorrow would be epic, she knew it. There were going to be twenty-five young minds in her charge that, not only could she mold them the way she wanted, but she'd learn a great deal too. Tisha loved being a teacher.

"Morning, Tisha. I have two boxes for you today." Taking them from Mildred, Tisha made her way to her room. Yesterday she'd started hanging the posters that she'd picked up here and there, and today she had her new teaching tools. The big box on her desk wasn't anything she'd seen before, but she paid no attention to it as she was eager to get the other two open.

The big clock, one that had numbers that were removable, was hung behind her desk. It was to help the second graders learn to tell time. Not that many people wore a watch or had

213

analog clocks anymore, but she was going to teach them.

The second box, much larger than the first, held the crayons that she'd begged for from the company that made them, as well as pencils and coloring books that she'd not expected. As she put them in the bins, each item having its own space, she glanced at the box on her desk. Whatever it was, it would have to wait until she got her long list finished.

Names were put on the desks, along with their cubbyhole assignment. The calendar with all the different seasons was hung low enough for little hands to change. It took her nearly an hour to mark the dates of each of their birthdays and to make sure that each name was spelled correctly. Nothing could be more embarrassing for a child then not having someone spell their name correctly.

Going to her car twice, she brought in bottled water that she'd purchased for her room. Hand-sanitizer in large bottles was placed around the room, along with rolls of paper towels. The second trip was for small gifts for jobs well done. Baggies for accidents that sometimes happened, as well as small supplies like Band-Aids, ice packs, and a few soft pillows. It was nearly nine-thirty that night, when she started for the door to go home, before she remembered the box.

Tisha wanted to go home. It was late, later than she'd thought she'd be here, and she was starving. The box, she decided, would have to wait. Whatever was in it, nothing that she could remember ordering anyway, would be there in the morning. She was nearly to her car when her cell phone went off.

"You have a good day tomorrow, love." Her dad could make even exhaustion go away when he called her. "I'm sure that you're going to have the best class, the prettiest room, and the most loving students."

"I'd love that. Very much so. And to be honest, I think I might have gone a little overboard with the room this year." He told her that wasn't possible as she leaned against her car to talk to him. Tisha did not use her phone and drive. "I got this strange box too. Did you send me anything?"

"No. Where did it come from, does it say?" She told him it only had a Post-it note on it with her name on it. "That's strange. Perhaps one of the other teachers gave you some extra they had."

That didn't sound right either. Most of the teachers were a good deal older than her, and usually did nothing to their room but what was required of them. Not that it was a bad thing…she liked most of them, but they'd never have any extras. And even if they did, they'd not share it if they could make a buck or two from it. The other teachers were barely making it on what they made each paycheck.

Tisha didn't need to work, she wanted to. And being a teacher was all she'd dreamed of since she was in first grade. She loved her job and all the perks more than she did anything in the world.

"Did I tell you I heard from Emma? She had a little girl." Her dad laughed and asked if she was a hellion like Emma's grandmother had been. "I would imagine. From the stories that she told me about her, I'd say Emma is hoping not. Grandma Emily was a pistol, I guess."

"You have no idea. That woman would cut you down with just a look and then drink you under the table. She wasn't one to hold grudges, nor did she know a stranger. I heard that she was having the time of her life when she finally passed on." Tisha had heard that as well. "So, are you going to go and visit her soon? I'd like to meet the man that finally tamed her."

"He's a cowboy." Her dad laughed. "Yeah, I thought that was funny too. He and his family own cattle of all things. And I guess one of them has a vineyard. She's going to send me a few bottles when they get them up and running."

She looked at the school again, wondering about that stupid box. Her dad would just tell her to go in and open it, but she really did want to get home. Getting in her car and putting on her seat belt, she told her dad that she needed to get home.

"All right, my dearest. You rest up for tomorrow, and don't forget to call me when you get home. Or even on a break. I'm curious to know what sort of children my little girl is going to be teaching." She promised that she would. "And sweetheart, you should come here soon. I miss you."

"I was just there last week, Dad. You can't miss me already." But she knew that he did because she missed him too. "I'll make some arrangements to come home next weekend. Okay?"

After ending the call, she started the car. For ten minutes she sat there thinking about the stupid box. Turning off the car, she made her way to the building again. The doors were locked.

"Decision taken from me."

Going to her car again, she decided that she'd come in early and open it then. Whatever it was, it had better be worth it, she thought, knowing that she wasn't going to get any sleep thinking about it.

Now Available in the Pride of the Double Deuce Series

Coming Soon

Before You Go...

HELP AN AUTHOR

write a review

THANK YOU!

Share your voice and help guide other readers to these wonderful books. Even if it's only a line or two your reviews help readers discover the author's books so they can continue creating stories that you'll love. Login to your favorite retailer and leave a review. Thank you.

AWARD WINNING, BESTSELLING AUTHOR

Kathi Barton, winner of the Pinnacle Book Achievement award as well as a best-selling author on Amazon and All Romance books, lives in Nashport, Ohio with her husband Paul. When not creating new worlds and romance, Kathi and her husband enjoy camping and going to auctions. She can also be seen at county fairs with her husband who is an artist and potter.

Her muse, a cross between Jimmy Stewart and Hugh Jackman, brings her stories to life for her readers in a way that has them coming back time and again for more. Her favorite genre is paranormal romance with a great deal of spice. You can visit Kathi on line and drop her an email if you'd like. She loves hearing from her fans. aaronskiss@gmail.com.

Follow Kathi on her blog: http://kathisbartonauthor.blogspot.com/